THAT MAN NEXT DOOR

NADIA LEE

FOUR ISLES PRESS

That Man Next Door

Copyright © 2017 by Hyun J Kyung

http://www.nadialee.net

1

I don't know what happened to Murphy to get a law named after him, but after today I'm pretty sure I deserve one, too.

Jan's Law. When you think things are going to be okay, shit goes down the toilet so fast you can't escape the funnel of poop before you hit raw sewage.

But I've finally reached the three-level, four-bedroom house in Dulles, Virginia I've shared with two of my closest friends since we graduated college almost four months ago. I'm not dead, so I'm going to consider this a win—even though I still deserve a law named after me.

"I'm home!" I call out as I drag my small black carry-on in, wheels rumbling on the hardwood floor.

Nobody greets me. I scowl. It's barely six on Sunday. I know at least one of my housemates is home because I saw Sammi's car in the driveway.

"You know, when somebody says, 'I'm home,'

you're supposed to say, 'welcome back!'" Somewhat peeved, I kick off my stilettos. I have no idea why I bothered with these abominations for my return trip home. It wasn't like I was going to run into One-Night Stand Number Five on my way to JFK, and it isn't like me to care what those guys think anyway. I always pick ones I'll never run into again because I've never had a successful one-night stand, the kind that goes all the way to the finale. I always get anxious and opt for Bailey.

But I panicked, worrying that I might bump into Number Five again before my trip was over—*I had this intuition, okay?*—so I put on the hooker heels and a skin-tight dress in the brightest shade of sunflower yellow. For some bizarre reason, I didn't want to face him in my comfy clothes. And I thanked every divinity in existence when I didn't run into him as I checked in for my flight at JFK, because I'm totally okay with my intuition being wrong.

And how did the universe reward me for my humble gratitude?

It bumped me off my ten thirty flight. Maybe I should count my blessings that I wasn't "reaccommo-dated" with a broken nose and a busted lip. Instead, I was placed between a manspreader and a heavy breather on a plane that idled for so long I could've done a mani-pedi and exfoliated every inch of my body while we were on the tarmac. During the flight the turbulence was so bad, the seat belt left bruises on my hips. Still...no scorpions dropped on my head, so I tried so very hard to consider the day a win. Because a girl's gotta be positive, right?

But no. The universe wasn't finished dumping on me.

My driver—can't even remember which company I picked for my ride home since I was too out of it by the time I deplaned—spotted his girlfriend laughing in a convertible with her ex and decided to give chase instead of taking me to my destination.

But somehow I made it. Home, sweet home. I plop myself on the dark brown leather massage chair. It's a gift from my grandmother. A nice, machine-induced relaxation session surrounded by the color of chocolate is exactly what I need to recover from the day's ordeal.

Just as I'm about to hit the full-body massage button, my best friend and housemate Sammi yells, "Hey, come here! You gotta see this!"

"It can wait." *After my massage.*

"No, it can't!"

I growl and push myself off the heavenly chair. Do I really want to join her? What if she's found a giant rat? Given my luck today, it'll probably have wings and a belt full of ninja stars to cut our faces.

I spot Sammi in the kitchen and stop. At five-foot six, she's slim from her daily morning runs. The only time she skips is when we have weather bad enough to ground planes or call FEMA. She wears unrelenting black from top to bottom because the object of her unrequited love once told her the color made her look chic, and today's no exception. Black tank top, black denim shorts. If her hair weren't naturally black, she'd dye it.

Sammi's staring out the window over the sink, her dark brown eyes unblinking as though she's mesmerized by what's on the other side. I make a face. It's six p.m., and that can only mean one thing. "When did you develop a fetish for a jiggly, naked hairy dude?"

"Like I said, you gotta see this," she says, pushing a flyaway out of her line of sight.

"No, thank you. I've seen ThaMaNDo more than enough."

"You only saw him that one time," she says.

"*Exactly.*" Once was more than enough, especially when we're talking about ThaMaNDo, a.k.a. *That Man Next Door*, as we dubbed him, since none of us was willing to strike up a conversation and ask him his name. Nope, no way.

He moved in ten days ago, having bought Mr. and Mrs. Jones's house after they retired and left for a sunny beach in Mexico. Normally I have no problem with our neighbors as most of them are nice people. But not ThaMaNDo. He has a nasty habit of dancing naked in his living room, which faces our kitchen, with the curtains open. It happens between six and seven p.m. every day, like clockwork. To be honest, calling what he does dancing is generous since it's more like a *grand mal* seizure, his whole flabby body jiggling and his stick and balls shaking like—

Well. Certain things are better left undescribed.

"It's not ThaMaNDo," Sammi says. "I saw him

4

drive off this morning with a couple of suitcases, and he hasn't been back since."

"Then who?"

She points. "Look!"

So I do, because I know she isn't going to tell me anything otherwise. And I swear to God, if Sammi's playing a joke on me and makes me see that fur-covered man in his birthday suit again, I'm going to kick her out. The house is mine—a legacy from my late mother—and the three of us are sharing it to cut costs. Even though I don't have a mortgage, there's insurance, taxes, upkeep and utilities. Besides, the house is way too big for a single gal. But I'll risk the added expense if Sammi makes me see what no human should ever have to...

Girding my loins, I squint out the window, then stop as I take in a new guy. This one's nothing like the previous ThaMaNDo. Facing away from the window, he's topless...and I have to say, I wouldn't complain if he showed a little more skin. His shoulders are broad and neatly muscled, and his torso tapers to a narrow waist and pelvis. His lats and traps are lean and well-defined, and a man who has a back like that always has an incredible body all over. A pair of threadbare jeans hugs his ass—and what a glorious ass it is.

"Damn," I mutter.

"Told you." Sammi smirks. "Why isn't *he* naked?" she complains, gesturing in the direction of his house.

"Stop being a hypocrite," I say in a mock stern voice.

"Me? A hypocrite? Since when?"

5

"Since you've been complaining about how unfair it is that so many games feature women who're barely dressed." And trust me, I had to hear about it for years since we roomed together in college, too.

Sammi waves me away. "That doesn't count. Those were just games. This is real life. Besides, he has no clue I'm over here objectifying him. What he doesn't know doesn't hurt him." She squints. "Wonder if his face is as yummy as his body."

"Hope so," I say. "Otherwise it'd be tragic."

"ThaYuMNDo could be related to ThaMaNDo," Sammi points out.

"Or not. ThaMaNDo's short." This divine man is not. Nope, he's at least six one. Maybe taller. He moves a few boxes, his back and arms flexing.

"Legit point. He also doesn't look like a werewolf in midshift."

I snort out a laugh, then fan my face. "Maybe I should join a local gym."

"Why? We get the company gym for free."

"But I can't ogle men there."

"Please. You can ogle men anywhere as long as they're single."

"Not coworkers." I shudder. "It makes me feel kind of guilty, like I'm violating HR policy."

"You probably are," Sammi agrees cheerfully, totally unsympathetic since she doesn't use the gym.

"If the local one has men half as good as this guy, it'll be worth the monthly fee."

"Just join a gay porn club. Cheaper and better

selection. No guarantee ThaMaNDo isn't a gym member."

I make a face. He's the last man I want to see.

Just then our new and much improved neighbor turns around. My mouth dries, all the thoughts in my head leaking out through my ears. Or at least that's how it feels. And my knees get jigglier than ThaMaNDo's belly.

The yummy man has the most perfect face, one I ran my lips all over. Thick black hair brushes his high and wide forehead, and a slight slant of straight eyebrows makes him appear serious yet slightly wicked at the same time. The deep-set eyes underneath are the most piercing blue. The blade of his nose is thin and straight, cheekbones model-high and his mouth...

Oh my God! That mouth. It whispered wicked things, nibbled and licked and kissed me until I felt like my whole body was about to burst into flame even as the flesh between my legs grew embarrassingly wet.

Heat floods my face, and I drop to the floor before he can see me in my ridiculous yellow dress. It practically screams, "See how awesome I look!"

Sammi glances down. "What's wrong?"

I cover my face. "Oh shit. Damn it. I'm so fucked."

"How? What are you talking about?"

"It's *him*."

"Who's him?"

"That man!" I flick my wrist behind me. "He's Number Five."

"*Damn*, girl! You sure know how to pick 'em!"

Sammi whistles, then waggles her eyebrows, squatting next to me. "So...a virgin no more?"

I purse my mouth. There's only one right answer here, and sadly I can't lie about it.

An embarrassed silence reigns in the kitchen. I finally look at my best friend.

Sammi stares at me as though I've sold my sanity to the lowest bidder on eBay. At long last she says, "*You Baileyed on him?*"

"Kinda..." Bailey is an app she and I created together in case we needed to get the hell out in the middle of a bad date. Or in my case, a one-night stand. It calls you at a predesignated time, and when you answer, it tells you in a chirpy female voice there's an emergency you have to attend to ASAP, thereby providing you with a graceful exit, no hard feelings. It's not available for download anywhere. We rooted our phones to install it.

Sammi's jaw drops. "*Why?*"

"Because!" I wail, then stop. I don't know why I did it. I shouldn't have. If I'm going to lose my V-Card, he's a great guy to do it with. But...

"Did he, like...smell?"

"No."

"Bad breath? Rotting teeth?"

"No. No." He has beautiful white teeth and the cutest dimple when he smiles. Just thinking about his facial architecture makes a sigh well up in my chest.

"Then what was the problem?"

"*I don't know!*" And that's the truth. I just couldn't do the deed.

"I can't believe you." Sammi shakes her head. "You're the only girl I know who's managed to keep her hymen intact after *five* one-night stands."

"Do they still count if I aborted in the middle?" I ask in a small voice.

"Of course they count." She crosses her arms. "So what are you going to do?"

"Stay down here until he goes home."

Sammi shakes her head, then throws her arms up. "What if that *is* his home?"

"Can't be. What about ThaMaNDo?" I never thought I would want that primate back, but I do. Desperately.

"Maybe he died." Sammi taps her pointed chin. "It's plausible that somebody brained him after getting tired of all that nude dancing. I'm sure it's legal."

"I'm pretty sure it isn't."

She keeps going. "Maybe ThaMaNDo and ThaYu-MNDo are housemates, and there'll be another chance for you two to hook up, assuming you don't Bailey on him again. I legit cannot believe you did that with such a prime specimen."

I cover my ears. I can't listen to her speculate anymore. This is my life.

"Do you at least know his name?" Sammi asks, tapping on my shoulder. "Not that I mind calling him ThaYuMNDo."

"Matt." Strong. Masculine. Just like the man himself.

Someone knocks at the door, and I jump up and run for it. Maybe it's a Jehovah's Witness. Or volunteers from my least favorite politician's campaign. I don't care. Anyone would be preferable to my best friend's inquisition into Botched One-Night Stand Number Five. The previous grillings weren't so bad, but then she never had a chance to see the men I bailed out on. And none of them were as scrumptious as Matt.

I'm about to open the door, but stop when Sammi glances out the kitchen window—which can also show you who's dropping by if you crane your neck extra hard—and calls, "Hottie alert! Stick your tits out!" in that exceptionally gleeful voice that makes my blood curdle.

I don't need to open it to know it isn't a Jehovah's Witness.

Jan's Law is still in effect.

Just in case Matt is a mutant alien with the power to see through doors, I cover my face and run back to the kitchen, while moaning deep in my throat like a wounded animal desperate to be put down, although the sound I make seems more similar to a rabid dog's. Ducking behind the marble-top counter, I clasp my hands together and pray I wake up now.

This has got to be a nightmare I'm having on my flight back home. Economy class comes with seats just big enough for an armless, legless prepubescent human. It makes sense that it also comes with dreams as dreadful as the seats. Is it too late to pay for an upgrade? I bet the first-class passengers don't doze off and dream about all the hotties they bailed on.

"Pussy," Sammi mutters under her breath, nudging my foot with hers. "Come on. He heard you run. You weren't exactly quiet."

I shake my head.

"Just face him," she says.

"No."

"God, you're a basket case." She sighs and heads for the door. "You fucking owe me."

"Thank you," I whisper. I do owe her. Big. At least a kidney.

"Hello, there," Sammi says, opening the door. "I'm Sammi, and you are...?"

"Matt," he says, his voice deep with the hint of rasp I found so irresistible in that bar in Manhattan. It still seems to scrape my nerve endings, sending warm tingles all over. "I just moved in over there."

I don't have to see him to know he is gesturing at the house. Shit. ThaMaNDo is definitely gone...or at least has a housemate.

"Great." Sammi beams. "Welcome to the neighborhood."

"And...if you don't mind, would it be okay if I borrowed some sugar?" he asks sweetly.

I wince. That's so cliché it hurts. Maybe he knew he would run into me. I mean... Why else would he come to this house rather than the other homes right around his?

"Sure you can...if you'll answer a few questions."

"Okay."

"Just to be clear, I already have a man I've set my sights on. They're really for my chickenshit friend."

"That's fine."

I scooch over a bit and use my compact mirror to spy on them, making sure it doesn't flash. Matt's smiling, showing that adorable dimple.

I bite my lower lip to contain a small whimper. My body remembers what he did right after he flashed that wicked smile and dimple on Friday. Unfulfilled need thrums in my blood, and it's all I can do to squat still.

"Are you in a committed relationship at the moment?" Sammi asks. "Wife, fiancée or girlfriend?"

My hand flies to my flaming cheek. I take it back. I do *not* owe her a kidney. What I owe her is a firm kick in the ass.

Matt blinks, then says, "Ah...no."

"Any children?"

"Nope."

"What's your IQ?"

A corner of his mouth curls upward, and he answers in that "I'm humoring you" tone, when he should be calling cops on my crazy best friend so she can be locked up. "At least three digits, although I wouldn't know for sure since I've never been tested."

"We'll go with one hundred twenty plus. You sound intelligent enough."

Sammi looks at the kitchen over a shoulder and grins that grin, and I know she's going to ask something super-embarrassing before this inquiry is over. She doesn't care what Matt thinks, and she is enjoying my discomfort entirely too much. I shake my head frantically, but not frantically enough since she ignores the palpable *nope* radiating through the counter in invisible waves.

She leans closer and lowers her voice. "Do you have any diseases?"

He cocks an eyebrow. "Diseases?"

"Yeah. You know. Like AIDS. Herpes. Genital warts. Syphilis. Cancer. The usual."

He coughs. Or maybe he's choking. It's hard to tell because blood is roaring in my head with murderous intent. Finally he says, "I'm clean. You want a doctor's note?"

"That won't be necessary, although you can drop off a copy if you like," she purrs.

"And you?"

"What about me?"

"Are you clean?"

"Oh, I'm not the one you should be worrying about." She chortles.

I'm going to kill her. If this isn't the most perfect justification for strangling your best friend, I don't know what is.

"Can I have that sugar?" he asks pointedly.

"Huh. So you really do need sugar?"

"I wouldn't have been answering your...*interesting* questions otherwise."

She nods. "Fair enough. Wait one second."

She comes to the kitchen with a black mug and gives me an "I did all the work for you" look, while filling his mug with some white sugar from the pantry.

I slash a finger across my neck, slowly, and she merely laughs.

Bitch.

She hands him the sugar, and he says, "Thanks," while giving her a curious look as he leaves.

I count to five after the door closes to make sure he's out of hearing range. Then I jump to my feet and face my best friend. "What the hell, girl!"

"What?" Sammi says.

"I can't believe you asked him those questions!"

"I was trying to help you out. He's too fine a specimen to bail out on. Now that he's proven to be intelligent, healthy and available—and without children—you can try one more time. You can even date him if he's good in the sack...and I bet he is."

"No."

Sammi wraps one arm around her belly, then rests the other elbow on it and props her chin in a hand. "Why not?"

"Because. The whole point of losing my virginity isn't to have a relationship."

"Then what is it about?"

"A milestone—something you do and then move on."

"That's crazy."

"Not any crazier than your insane questions! Wife?

Fiancée? Girlfriend? Children? Diseases? Oh my God!"

Sammi spreads her arms. "You're welcome! If you're peeved about not asking for a doctor's note, just let me know and I'll ask next time I see him."

I tilt my head back, staring at the ceiling. "I hate you."

"I expect you to make me your maid of honor. I totally have a feeling about you two."

2

After a quick shower to wash away the grime from my travels, I start to feel a bit better. Maybe I overreacted. Sammi means well, and she's been trying to get me to loosen up and get rid of my V-Card, assuming I can find a worthy man.

I change into a loose T-shirt and yoga pants and go down for dinner. It's probably what the doctor ordered. Food always improves my mood, the junkier the better.

"I bring pizza!" announces Michelle as she walks in, carrying a huge Costco pizza box. Her hooker shoes click on the hardwood floor, and she kicks them off by the door, wriggling her toes. Her carefully styled brown hair is more wavy than curly now, and the makeup on her face is flawless, bringing out her wide-set caramel-colored eyes and high cheekbones. Crimson red coats her bee-stung lips—all the guys in my dorm called them DSL—and a low-cut, skimpy black dress shows off her pushup bra-enhanced cleavage.

"Perfect timing," I say with a grin. "I was just thinking about grabbing something to eat."

"Sammi told me to get it on the way, saying you'd need it."

I make a face. "At least she knows how to atone for her sins."

"What happened?" She dumps her purse on the couch and sets the pizza on the dining table, big enough for six.

"We have a new neighbor."

"ThaMaNDo is gone, replaced by ThaYuMNDo," Sammi says as she joins us. "How was your day?"

"Quite good. Nabbed a cheater." Michelle grins triumphantly. Although she works at Sweet Darlings Inc. like me and Sammi, she also moonlights as a honeypot for a local PI on weekends. Young and gorgeous, she makes perfect bait.

We settle at the dining table and each grab a slice. After a big bite, Michelle says, "So. Who's this ThaYuMNDo?"

And of course Sammi tells her everything, starting with my failed One-Night Stand Number Five and ending with the humiliating inquisition.

"Wow. That's...something," Michelle says.

"I know, right?" I take a big swallow of Coke. "She went too far."

Michelle nods. "Could've been more subtle for sure. And the question about the diseases was pointless. Guys lie about that all the time. Hell, they lie about their relationship status all the time too."

"Don't let your job turn you cynical. He seemed pretty sincere," Sammi says with a careless shrug. "It's important for him to know we care about stuff like that."

Michelle chews her food contemplatively. "You should just tell him."

"What?" I say.

"That you're interested in finishing what you started."

"Can't do that."

"Why not?"

"Because he moved in next door," I say.

"But that's perfect. You can keep an eye on him. Go for a second helping if the first is good."

Sammi nods. "Multiple helpings are always convenient, especially when it's next door."

"Like a buffet," Michelle says.

"Exactly. An 'all you can fuck' neighbor."

"But I don't want to keep an eye on him or have multiple helpings," I say. "I never wanted to see him again."

Michelle blinks. "Really?"

"Why do you think I only try one-night stands when I'm out of town?"

"I thought it was the hotel room making you frisky. Hotel rooms bring that out in people."

"It isn't about the room."

"Apparently there's a milestone to be achieved," Sammi says drily.

Michelle gives me a wide-eyed look. She probably

thinks I'm insane, but then she never had the problem I have with her own V-Card. "So what are you going to do? You can't avoid him forever now that we're neighbors."

"We avoided running into ThaMaNDo," I point out.

"Yeah, but only because he never went to work in the morning like the rest of us." Sammi taps the rim of her glass thoughtfully. "ThaYuMNDo looks like he's gainfully employed."

He probably is. He told me he was a lawyer when we met. But then he also told me he lived in New York. Liar. "I'm going to make sure to leave for work an hour early."

Michelle shudders. To her, sleep is sacrosanct. "And how long is this going to last?"

"Until he moves!"

3

The next morning I get up an hour early. And to make sure I don't run into Matt, I move fast. After a quick shower, I apply some makeup and pull my flaming red hair into a tight bun. I wish I had black hair like Sammi, but there's nothing to be done about it. To disguise my face further, I even put on a pair of Clark Kent glasses I borrowed from Michelle. I'm not naïve enough to believe they can fool Matt into believing I'm someone I'm not—that only works in comic books—but he probably won't be able to tell who I am from a distance.

I hope.

I sigh wistfully. A pair of sunglasses would be better, but I left mine on the plane. I'm ninety-nine percent sure I won't see them again. I should go buy another pair this afternoon.

And for extra insurance, I slip on my lucky underwear—the lacy barely-there stuff I bought on a shopping excursion with Michelle. She's of the opinion that the type of underwear you put on in the morning can make or break your day, and although I don't subscribe to the belief the way she does, a little extra insurance can't hurt.

I wear a beige fitted top and conservative gray pencil skirt, plus very un-hookerish ballet flats in black. They couldn't be more different from my Project Lose V-Card outfits. Even my purse is a sedate black Coach I picked up on sale at an outlet store.

By the time I walk out the door, Michelle's alarm is going off, and Sammi returns from her run, her entire body dripping with sweat. The black Nike tights and workout tank top look sleek on her, and she sucks down some water before saying, "You weren't kidding about getting up early."

"Nope."

She shakes her head. "Way too much work to avoid that prime piece. You should tap that fine ass. There are worse ways to lose your V-Card." She slips inside, ignoring my face.

Matt's car—a metallic red BMW convertible—sits in the driveway. Unless I'm mistaken the man's not up yet. All the curtains and blinds are drawn, and I don't see any lights inside.

Maybe I'll get lucky, and it'll turn out that Matt works at night...although I'm not certain what kind of lawyer works a graveyard shift. But you never know these days, right? The business world doesn't sleep anymore. He could be working for a giant conglomerate in Beijing or something to iron out some huge deal that will make or break the CEO's bonus for the year.

And if he doesn't work eight to five, I can start getting up at my normal time. The lack of sleep—even just one hour—is hitting me hard, and I really need a caffeine boost.

For some reason, there's no line at the local Starbucks drive-through. Does this mean my luck's improving?

What goes down must come up. Surely my luck hit rock bottom last night, and today's going to be one big universe song saying, "Sorry, girl, lemme make it up to you."

I can totally get behind that.

I get a Grande caramel macchiato with full-fat milk. Normally I get a Venti with skim, but I deserve to splurge for getting up early.

Then...because I feel extra lucky today, I stop by a local gas station and buy a lottery ticket. My chances of winning the jackpot—currently worth more than fifty million bucks—are so slim, a Boeing Triple Seven's more likely to drop on me first. But hey, a girl can dream, even though I don't have the slightest clue what I would do if I actually won.

Probably breathe into a paper bag, then put the money away somewhere and go back to work. And attempt One-Night Stand Number Six.

The drive to Sweet Darlings Inc. doesn't take more than ten minutes. Even during rush hour, it's only twenty minutes from my house. The headquarters is a beautiful fifteen-story ivory square building located in Sweetridge, a subdivision in Dulles. When my grandmother, Alexandra Darling, started the company, the area was relatively inexpensive and not as developed. She managed to poach plenty of programming talent from AOL and government contractors who wanted to do something more fun and interesting. Over the years, she's shifted her core business focus from desktop publishing to a sleek mobile app that people can use to share their most treasured memories. Our original, and still the biggest and most responsive, target audience is new parents. On average, each user spends over three hundred dollars a year to preserve and share pictures and videos of their babies. And we have teams dedicated to meet all their wants.

I reach the fourteenth floor and walk toward my desk, which is right outside the corner office of marketing manager David Darling, who also happens to be my cousin. My workstation is modest, with an L-shaped wooden desk and three filing cabinets. Although the company has technically gone paperless, in reality, we still produce a lot of paper in the marketing division. On my desk is a small faux-metal plaque with my name on it: Jan Doe. There's no title on the bottom, unlike the one on David's door.

I place my purse in the bottom drawer and lock it,

then boot my laptop. An email program launches automatically and downloads emails.

"Good morning, Jan."

I look up at my grandmother's serene greeting. She's dressed fashionably as usual in a light coral sweater dress and nude patent leather flats. Her formerly auburn hair has gone completely steel gray now. Although she refuses to dye it, she indulges in an expensive bob that looks elegant and fluffy around her egg-shaped face. Her thin lips are curved into a small smile that doesn't show any teeth—she never shows them, although she has all her real teeth—and her pale gray eyes warm as she looks at me.

"You're in early," I say.

"I'm always in around this time."

"Oh." That's news to me. I always assumed she got in when she got in, since she's the CEO and chairperson of Sweet Darlings Inc., not to mention she'll be sixty-five in less than a week. Who's going to give her a hard time about coming in after nine?

"You, on the other hand, *are* early," she says. "Nice glasses."

"I have some things to catch up on," I fib. There's no way I'm telling her about my One-Night Stand Number Five. I clear my throat. "Thank you."

"I hope you can spare a moment, though."

"Of course." My grandmother or not, Alexandra is the head of the company. She doesn't give anyone any slack, not even her own children. It prevents others from feeling resentful.

She leans on the edge of my desk. "I'm not sure if you saw, but we have openings on the app development team and some managerial tracks."

"I read the email last week." HR sends opening announcements to all employees.

"Are you going to apply?"

"Um. I haven't given it any thought." *No.*

"You should. They're great opportunities for you."

"I'm sure they are."

She regards me steadily. "You aren't going to do it."

"I'm really busy these days, and the applications take a while."

"It's a worthwhile effort. Many positions are entry level, and you're eminently qualified."

"I didn't know that. I thought they wanted someone with more experience," I lie. "I'll check the listings again later today."

"Please do." Alexandra straightens. "I see great potential in you, my dear."

"Thank you." But I don't call her "grandma." Sometimes I'm not sure which Alexandra Darling I'm talking to.

"And don't forget the party on Saturday. You can bring a date if you want. And then take the boxes afterward."

"I won't forget." The party is to celebrate her upcoming birthday, and everyone in the family is required to attend. "And I will, if I find anybody suitable." I make no comment about the boxes of Mom's stuff in Alexandra's attic because I don't want to get into it first thing in the morning.

She tilts her head and looks at me as though she's worried. She shouldn't be. "Have a productive day."

"You, too."

Alexandra leaves, and I turn to my laptop and click through my messy inbox. The email from HR catches my attention, probably because of my chat with Grandma. The app dev position looks über-interesting. The team's very small and dedicated to leveraging our free users by serving them ads that they find relevant and meaningful. The entire point of our free app is that we don't spam or bother our users with intrusive junk that nobody wants, but still manage to monetize them.

If interested, apply here the big yellow button says. My mouse cursor hovers over it...but then I sigh and click on an email regarding a new campaign David's team's working on instead. Alexandra's been trying to steer me away from administrative positions, but I don't want to squeak onto the team because of her desire to see me do something more important than keep David's schedule or make photocopies for meetings. All of my uncles and aunts and cousins are in management, but they were born for that kind of stuff.

What about me, you ask?

Well, I'm not even really wanted by the Darling family. They didn't know I existed until my mom died in a car crash when I was ten, and they *had* to take me in. But I know my place. I'm the kid who shouldn't have been conceived, because without me, my mom might've gone back home and not died like that. Nobody in the Darling family is crude or ungracious enough to say it out loud, but I can put two and two together. Mom was the youngest of Alexandra's five children—and the only girl to boot. She ran off with my dad when she was eighteen, against Alexandra's explicit orders to stay away from him. Apparently it was infatuation at first sight. Then she got pregnant with his child—me.

She never revealed who he was, and she never married him. I don't know if they split while she was pregnant or not. She told me he was a great man, but then it's in all moms' job descriptions to say stuff like that to their kids. I'm not stupid enough to think anything my mom did with my dad was for love, though, because on my birth certificate she wrote down "John Doe" for father. If she loved him, she would've told him or his family, and I would've met my paternal grandparents. She also pretended like she had no family, although she never lacked for money, as she had a modest trust from her late father. (I found out about the trust only after I turned twenty-one, and Alexandra gave me the house she bought with the fund as an investment.)

As for me? I'm supposed to be Jane Doe—I'm certain of it—but Mom never bothered to correct the clerical error, so I'm just Jan.

My throat suddenly dries, and I take a big gulp of my macchiato. I shouldn't be that upset about my mom being lazy. Just imagine the kind of ridicule I would've suffered growing up if my name had been Jane Doe.

Jan Doe is a great name. Mom was being considerate by letting the error stand. I take another sip of my drink and start to attack the daunting number of emails in my inbox. I'm not going to feel sorry for myself, not when I have a house, a job and great friends.

4

In about an hour, the office comes to life as my coworkers begin to arrive and the distinct aroma of freshly brewed coffee permeates the place. Grandma doesn't believe in cheap java for her staff. The carefully ground, organic beans come from plantations overseas where growers practice sustainable and responsible farming.

My phone buzzes. It's Loretta from reception. She and I have been close since we went through orientation together and were in the same group for the team building exercises.

–Loretta: Fresh donut alert!

I raise my eyebrows.

–Jan: What's the occasion?

–Loretta: A new hire. Wow. He's hot. Hope he's not taken or gay. The good ones are never available.

I take this with a couple cups of salt. She's on the

rebound and desperate to hook up—any halfway decent guy would do.

—Jan: That's how you know they're good. A hottie who isn't taken yet? Weird.

—Loretta: Somebody has to be the first. >:(Why can't it be me?!

I can feel a palpable pout through the text, which is no minor feat.

—Jan: Somebody usually is the first, except it only happens while the good ones are jailbait.

—Loretta: I know. I'm still bitter about breaking up with my first boyfriend. Do you know he's now worth at least ten million and totally hot?

—Jan: There'll be other chances...just not with somebody at the company. If anything goes wrong, it'll be more awkward and embarrassing than having a strip of toilet paper trailing out of your panties.

—Loretta: LOL.

I spot the tall, dark head of David moving my way. Twenty-nine years old, he's probably going to be somebody big and important at Sweet Darlings Inc. He's too smart and driven not to succeed, and he loves his job. He's in a blue dress shirt and black slacks, no tie. He hates ties, calling them socially mandated nooses.

—Jan: Boss sighting. Gotta go.

I put away my phone and smile. "Good morning, David."

"Morning." His gray gaze drops to the stack of paper on my desk. "You're in early."

"Decided to get a jump-start on the day!"

As he enters his office, I get up and start toward the break room. He told me I didn't have to, but I always get him a fresh coffee when he arrives because everyone else's assistant does. As bosses go, he's not bad...although he does take me into important meetings and then ask me to give input, even though I'm just an assistant and he knows I don't enjoy speaking up in front of everyone. He also works me hard, making me study and analyze data on our customer base. Sometimes I end up writing more memos on our audience segmentation than the analysts on our marketing team. There are times when I wonder if he's secretly hazing me.

About halfway there, I spot a dark-haired guy in a well-fitted navy pinstriped suit with a box of donuts. Must be the new hire Loretta was talking about. I can see why she went on about him in such an admiring way. The clothes fit his broad shoulders and lean torso perfectly, and although the jacket hides his butt from view, it's obvious from the way his slacks skim over the lean lines of his legs that he has one extraordinary ass.

He's facing away from me, chatting with Cora Darling, another of my cousins. She's in finance. Unlike her older sister, who's a model in New York City, Cora believes in sugar and fat with extra gluten. In spite of her love of junk food, she's slim with superb bone structure, having inherited both from her parents. Combined with glossy black hair and bright amber eyes, she's probably the best-looking woman in the building.

I pour a big mugful of fresh coffee for David, dump in a packet of Splenda—which is exactly how he likes it —then walk back to my desk to pick up a folder with the week's agenda and a few items he needs to review. The new hire's no longer at Cora's desk, probably having served her the donut of her choice.

Smart man. Fresh donuts are a cheap way to introduce and endear yourself to other people on the floor.

Cora notices me and gestures me over. I go, keeping an eye on the coffee to make sure it stays hot and fresh. As much as I love Cora, she can be a bit long-winded when she gets on a roll, and I can tell she's bursting with things to say.

She leans closer. "Have you met the new hire?"

"Not yet."

"You should."

"To get myself a donut?" I tease.

"No, silly. I mean, yeah, his donuts are great too. And you really should get one before all the good ones are gone."

"I thought all donuts are equally good."

"Nope. The best ones come with extra gluten and chocolate filling." She winks.

I giggle at how incorrigible she is. Her anti-healthy diet is partly a rebellion against her older sister, who's so healthy it's sickening. How much juiced kale can one ingest in a day without throwing up?

"But forget the donuts. Even if there aren't any left, you should still go see him. Just to check him out. That is one fine man. If I'd known that we'd replace Dick

Button with a guy this hot, I would've campaigned for him to retire sooner."

"So he's the new in-house counsel?"

"Yup."

Fascinating. I'd heard that we hired a new one, but I didn't know he was attractive enough to make Cora notice. She's really picky about men, but then she can afford to be. "I'll try to run into him if I can. Gotta go though. David's waiting for his coffee."

She wrinkles her nose. "I don't know why you bother. He should be getting his own."

"I don't mind. Gives me a chance to get away from my desk." And a steady supply of caffeine keeps him happy.

On my way to David's office, I grab the folder from my desk. I knock once and enter without waiting for an answer.

I stop so abruptly that I almost spill the coffee on my hand. I must be hallucinating because there's no way Matt, a.k.a. One-Night Stand Number Five, can be seated here. To clear my vision, I blink a few times. But nope. He's still in front of me, in one of the two chairs reserved for visitors.

Unlike before, he's in a suit—a navy pinstriped suit. There's a box of donuts, and...

"Oh, great," David says perkily. "Jan, meet Matt Aston. He's our new in-house counsel."

My gaze swings his way, then back at Matt. The hot guy Loretta and Cora were talking about. Of course. My brain scrambles to keep up, because how the hell do you think when your lungs are struggling to draw in enough air, and all you can hear is a loud roar in your head?

Without handing over the coffee, I turn right around and leave, letting the door close behind me with a click. Then I gulp in some air, my mouth moving like a goldfish's.

My new reality starts to sink in slowly.

Holy mother of God! Number Five is the new hire? What the hell am I going to do?

Is there anything I can do?

I think over the staccato beating of my heart. There's no reason to panic. Yes, ideally we would never see each other again, but this isn't a total disaster. I introduced myself on Friday using my one-night stand persona—Bella from Maryland who moved to Brooklyn three years ago. And Bella wore a skintight dress and hooker heels and her hair was wild and curled, her face fully made-up with bold colors I never use otherwise. I, as Jan Doe, look totally different in glasses and with my hair knotted tightly at my nape. Even my outfit's professional and on the conservative side. He might think I look similar to the girl he almost slept with, but so what? It's not like he's going to ask, "Hey, are you the girl who went down on me Friday night, and then left?"

Besides, he got to come. So what does he have to complain about?

"Um. Jan, are you okay?" comes David's voice over the intercom on my desk.

Crap. I grab a pen from my desk, stick it into the

folder and return to the office. "Sorry about that," I say with a broad smile and hand the coffee to David. "Had to go get my lucky pen." I take the only empty seat left, right next to the one Matt is occupying.

"I didn't know you had a lucky pen," David says.

"Well, I do," I say, twirling it around.

"That's a Bic from the supply room."

Oh shut up, shut up. I put the end in my mouth and bite until my teeth cut into the plastic. "There. The mark of luck."

My cousin gives me a look that says, "I don't get women," while Matt's studying me. I avoid looking at him, even though I can feel the weight of his gaze skimming over me from top to bottom, then back up, leaving my body hyperaware.

But keeping my eyes off him doesn't insulate me from his aftershave, which smells expensive and incredibly sexy. He had the same scent mingled with a hint of musky male and soap when we first met.

Warmth unfurls in my belly. *Why does he have to smell so divine?* I stay rigid so I don't squirm. Stick to the plan, I tell myself while adjusting my glasses.

"Anyway," David begins, "Matt, this is my assistant and cousin, Jan Doe. And Jan, in case you missed my earlier intro, this is Matt Aston, the new in-house counsel. He's a good friend of mine from Harvard, and I couldn't be happier that he's joining us."

Can my life get any worse? Matt isn't some random guy from New York City. He's David's *good* friend. I wonder if Alexandra knows him, too. At the rate things are going, the answer's going to be yes because Jan's Law is still in effect.

I inhale, then face Matt since there's no way to avoid him without looking rude. He gives me a megawatt smile, probably the kind reserved for occasions like crushing his enemies, except I'm not a courtroom nemesis. There's a speculative gleam in his sharp blue gaze that makes me wonder if he already knows everything, but that's an absurd assumption.

He extends a hand. I stare at it a beat longer than is polite. America's supposed to be this big melting pot... yet we haven't adopted the Asian custom of bowing to each other. That's surely better than touching skin-to-skin.

Come on, Jan. You're playing a woman who just met a guy.

Wishing I had Michelle's acting skills, I shake his hand. His palm is dry and warm, and he pumps firmly and confidently, just like the way he moved...

My cheeks heat. *Stop thinking about that night!*

A corner of his lips lifts for a second. Wait. Did he just smirk?

Before I can process what it means, Matt offers me a donut. There are still plenty left in the box. I grab a glazed one with chocolate filling because if I'm going to suffer through this, a treat is the least I deserve. "Thanks," I say.

"My pleasure."

I raise an eyebrow and peer at him over the rim of

my glasses. Did I imagine it, or was there that satisfied kitten-like purr to his tone?

"So how was your weekend?" Matt asks.

I almost choke on the donut, but catch myself. "It was great. I went shopping." Men hate hearing about shopping. Now the convo about my weekend is finished.

"How's Kathleen?" David asks.

Or not. "You know how she is. Always doing fantastic," I say.

"Does she work here too?" Matt asks.

"No," I say, leaving it at that.

David of course ruins it by adding, "She's a model now. Very busy. We almost never see her unless we go to New York."

God. I could kill David with my bare hands. Or at least I should start spitting in his coffee. Why does he have to air our family stuff in front of the company's in-house counsel?

I mean Kathleen being a model is totally cool, but Matt doesn't need to know what she does or—more importantly—where she lives.

The donut tastes like an inner tube filled with toothpicks, and is about as comfortable to swallow with my mouth so dry. This is why I don't lie—at least not to people I'm going to see again. When I get found out I can't just brazen my way through the way Michelle can.

I stand up, placing the folder on David's desk. "Please review this," I say, although my voice is too hoarse for my liking. "Excuse me." I spin around and leave.

On my way to the bathroom, I grab my phone. This calls for an emergency regrouping session.

Sitting on one of the toilets, I text Sammi and Michelle.

–Jan: You won't believe what just happened!

A few seconds later, I get a response.

–Sammi: What?

–Jan: ThaYuMNDo is here!

–Michelle: Aren't you at work?

–Jan: Yes. But he's here. He's Dick's replacement!

–Michelle: Dick from legal?

Is she serious? She's Miss HR. She should know there are no other replaced Dicks.

–Jan: YES!

–Michelle: Does this mean you don't have to get up early now?

I drop my head. I can't believe what she's focused on.

–Jan: That is so not the point!

–Michelle: What is the point?

–Sammi: Look, you walked out on the prime piece, so you gotta own it.

–Michelle: Yup. I mean, unless the guy's a rapist or something, he knows a woman can change her mind. He won't hold it against you.

–Sammi: He better not. I gotta go. Meeting in ten. Chat after work? I have a working lunch.

–Michelle: So do I. You joining us today?

–Sammi: For gossip? Hell yeah!

I sigh. At least my sex life—or lack thereof—merits Sammi joining us at the state-of-the-art company gym. Michelle and I do yoga there four times a week, and Sammi never bothers since she's already in such great shape.

I flush the toilet, sacrificing gallons of water at the altar of not looking weird. Maybe if I were more brazen, the way Sammi is, I could just walk out, not caring if anybody notices I didn't flush. But I don't want anybody to wonder why I was in the stall for so long without having the appropriate...you know...movements.

Izzy Friday from accounting glances at me when I start washing my hands. Twenty-seven years old, she's the biggest gossip in the entire building, and there's nothing that escapes the owlish brown eyes peering out from under her licorice-colored bangs. I honestly have no clue how she has time for her own life plus tracking everyone else's, but somehow she manages. Must be her extraordinary attention to detail. Too bad she doesn't apply that to accounting. She isn't the best accountant we have at Sweet Darlings Inc. I overheard Alexandra complain about her work once.

"Hey, girl," she says, looking at me in the mirror. "Have you checked out our new legal dick?"

"His name is Matt," I point out.

She undoes an extra button on her pale yellow blouse, then puts a hand inside to push her tits up, creating a more pronounced cleavage, the kind you can stick a wad of cash into and never see it again. "I know, but everyone in legal is a dick, so..." She giggles, adjusting her skirt to make it appear shorter. "But if every dick looked like that, who cares, right?"

I force a smile, although it annoys me she's talking about Matt like this—a piece of meat to be pursued. He isn't mine, and certainly any woman can date him, but not Izzy. "Aren't you dating somebody?"

"Nah. We're just fucking, nothing serious, but only because he's better than my B.O.B." She applies a fresh coat of bright red lipstick, then turns to me. "What do you think?"

"Looks nice," I say with less than full enthusiasm. The shade is dramatic with her pixie face and dark coloring.

Apparently oblivious to my mood, she turns back to the mirror. "More than nice. I had pink before, but it just doesn't highlight the pucker, you know?"

"Are you going to do Matt while you're seeing your other guy?"

"Why not? Neither of them will care. Men love sex, and I bet Matt never goes a night without getting laid...unless maybe he's sick."

She's making *me* sick with her commentary...but she's probably right. I'm sure Matt doesn't lack for fuck buddies if that's what he wants. Look how easily he got me into his hotel room, and I'm probably the only one from that encounter fretting about...

You know, I don't even know exactly *what* I'm

worried about regarding that particular incident. And that only makes me more annoyed.

It annoys me I didn't just go all the way like I should have, because I lost my chance with Matt.

It annoys me that I can't seem to want a relationship.

And it annoys me I can't take sex casually, like so many women do.

It's not even that I have some deep, religious or moral reason for my reluctance. I have no problem with sex in general, and I'm not particularly religious either, although I am spiritual. But sex to me isn't just sex. It's a risk.

A risk that I may become infatuated.

A risk that I might do something stupid, like get pregnant with the wrong guy's baby.

A risk that I might end up hurting the people who matter the most.

Just like my mom.

That's why even though I'm a virgin and don't need it to regulate my period or anything like that, I'm fanatical about birth control. I take mine every morning at seven thirty like clockwork. But somehow that's not enough because I keep thinking that it's not foolproof. It can fail. It *has* failed countless other women.

"What do you think?" Izzy is looking at me expectantly.

I stare at her. She looks like a young woman on the prowl to get laid, not an accountant at work on a

Monday, but I'm sure that isn't what she's asking. "Huh?"

She rolls her eyes. "You've been daydreaming, haven't you? Ugh. I wanted to know if you could get me an invite to Alexandra's birthday party."

"Why do you want to go?" Izzy doesn't work closely with my grandmother, and she doesn't know any of my cousins that well.

"To network. Rub elbows. I mean, all the people who matter from the company are going to be there."

"Yeah, like the C-suite guys, which is going to be boring. And the family, who have to be there. It's just a birthday get-together, no big deal, and it's going to be too crowded if she invites everyone from work," I say, trying to downplay the party. Knowing Grandma, the event's going to be great with fantastic music, amazing food and even better company. "The really big one is the party on Friday." Her assistant is planning a secret ceremony for Alexandra in the office. Well. "Secret"... but I'm sure my grandmother already knows about it. Nothing escapes her notice.

I clear my throat. "Anyway, I need to go. Got a meeting with David," I lie. Otherwise Izzy will never shut up. She's like a beady-eyed octopus intent on prey when she's found someone to gossip with.

She shrugs. "That's too bad. Have fun."

I give her a smile—or at least I hope it's a smile, since I bared my teeth and curved my lips. Then I make a big loop to avoid legal, which is located right smack between finance and marketing on this floor.

If I get super-lucky, Matt will be assigned to the legal team up on the fifteenth floor. But the universe is still being a rude bitch, continuing from yesterday, and I bet the fifty million dollar jackpot I'll never win that ThaYuMNDo is on my floor.

5

Sammi, Michelle and I don't get to gossip after work. Sammi's team has some kind of emergency, and Michelle's talk with her boss runs late. So I do yoga by myself since there's no reason to skip a workout. Alexandra is big on staying fit, and she insists that everyone in the family exercises regularly.

You think she won't know and skip a session...and then she'll mention it the next time you see her. It's really creepy. There's gotta be a secret camera installed in the company gym so she can keep track of what we're up to at all times. She's probably bugged our cars and homes too. She has info not even the NSA is privy to.

As I wipe my face with a towel and suck down some water, I wonder if she knows about my one-night stands. Ugh. I hope not. Talk about embarrassing! Besides, her knowing stuff is another good reason—

albeit a minor one—to pick up men far from northern Virginia.

"Hi, Jan."

I choke, then sputter. Half the water in my mouth ends up on my shirt, making it stick to my chest. A big, warm hand pats my back gently, making my sweat-misted skin prickle deliciously even through my workout shirt.

"You okay?" Matt peers at me.

"I'm fine," I croak out, looking back at him. Of all the things in the world. "Why are you here?" I immediately cringe at asking a question with such an obvious answer. His black hair is spiked with sweat, and his skin is damp. The Nike workout shirt and shorts he's wearing cling to the well-defined muscles underneath. What a waste that I can't see his bare abs. They are stunning—hard and ridged. I ran my fingertips all over them, marveling at their magnificence.

"David and I decided to catch a workout."

"Oh. Good for you," I say since I can't think of anything else.

"Contacts?"

"What?" I suddenly realize I'm not wearing the Clark Kent glasses. Oh crap! "My vision's not that terrible." Actually my vision's perfect, thank you very much, but I can't just tell him that, can I?

He tilts his head, his gaze sharp as he takes in my features. I flush under the scrutiny and wipe my face again, trying to hide behind the towel. "Gosh, I'm so hot and sweaty." The second I blurt it out, I could almost kill myself. Why don't I just add, "Gosh, I'm horny and wet too," while I'm at it?

Something wicked and searing gleams in his eyes. "Uh-huh. You look like you're having fun."

"I should shower." I gesture at the locker room. "I've got dinner plans."

His stare grows more intense—or am I just imagining things because I'm getting tenser and tenser the longer we talk? A small muscle in his jaw ticks before he finally says, "A date?"

"Yes. Most definitely," I say quickly. "Today is Mexican Monday with the girls."

A smile quirks his lips. "I thought that was supposed to be Taco Tuesday."

"Why limit it to Tuesdays when you can do it whenever you want?" Now I'm babbling. "Gotta go."

I bolt to the women's locker room before he can say anything else and rush through the shower. I need to join a local gym, not to ogle men, but for my own sanity. I should've known he'd be at the gym. He didn't get that body from writing legal briefs!

Although he might've gotten his forearms that way. Girl, you should've licked them when you had the chance, my most definitely worthless mind whispers.

I leave the gym, the glasses back on, my gaze straight, looking forward. Okay, not that forward. I surreptitiously glance around for Matt, and I see him finishing benching with David, pumping some serious poundage from the number of plates on each side of the barbell. I'm not the only woman who's checking him out.

He lifts his head as though he feels my gaze, and our eyes meet. My mouth dries, my cheeks going red again.

This totally proves Sammi's theory of optimal virginity disposal timing: If you don't lose it before finishing college, it's only going to get harder. But I'm still an honorary student, right? I only graduated this year.

I text my friends.

–Jan: Are we still going to Carlos's today?

–Michelle: Of course. I already made a reservation for 7 p.m.

–Sammi: On my way. Diving.

–Michelle: What?

–Sammi: Driving.

–Jan: Why are you texting?

–Sammi: Dictating. This newt app is wonky.

–Jan: Stop dictating.

–Sammi: Nude app. New. Duck it! I give up.

–Michelle: Just drive. You're gonna get yourself killed.

–Sammi: Red light. Chill.

–Michelle: See you in twenty.

Carlos's is a fantastic local Mexican restaurant about twenty minutes away from Sweet Darlings Inc. A lot of people from the company like to go after work, especially on Mondays because of their Margarita

Monday Specials. You can never say no to a five-dollar margarita.

When I finally pull into the lot in front of Carlos's, I feel almost normal again. The lack of a red BMW among the parked cars helps. Matt's probably still working out with David. Then I remember what Izzy said in the bathroom, and I wonder if she's at the gym flirting, that shameless hussy.

Nah. She's too lazy to work out. I've never seen her down there. On the other hand, she might go just to check him out. Loretta, too. She's definitely looking for a hookup to get over her ex. I bet they're "jogging," their eyes on his superbly defined arms and chest...and abs...and...

Gripping the steering wheel, I thump my forehead against my knuckles. Ugh. I'm being stupid. I already decided I don't want a relationship, so I should forget about Matt. He's a complication, and who wants to run into their one-night stand over and over again at work? Kind of defeats the purpose.

Also, Grandma frowns on interoffice dating in general, equating it to taking a dump where you dine. I don't want to give her any further reason to be disappointed with me.

I'm going to the Bay Area early next year with David to visit our San Mateo office. I should definitely find someone there. Someone who won't be popping up next door...or at our headquarters in Dulles.

Inhaling deeply, I stiffen my spine and get out of the car, then walk inside. The hostess recognizes me immediately and gives me a welcoming smile. "Your friends are already here." Sure enough, Michelle is waving from our favorite booth in the back.

I sit, putting my purse next to me, as our regular server, Diego, brings three margaritas.

"Just in time!" Michelle says.

"We have nachos too," Sammi says. She's obsessed with nachos. If she could, she'd eat them for breakfast.

I take a big gulp of the refreshingly cold margarita. I so deserve this after how life has been going since my latest ill-fated one-night stand.

"The usual, ladies?" Diego asks.

"Yes," I say.

Michelle nods, and Sammi gives him a thumbs up.

Our usual is pretty standard. I get a cheesy chicken burrito with guacamole, Michelle some triple beef tacos and Sammi seafood fajitas with two extra tortillas.

"Why do you look so morose?" Michelle asks after Diego leaves. She takes a quick selfie with her margarita—if you upload shots like that to Instagram and tag Carlos's, you can get prizes and coupons. "We're about to eat, and we got our discount alcohol."

"Probably low blood sugar," Sammi remarks, shoving a chip with extra melted cheese and salsa into her mouth.

I take a bite of the nachos. "Do we still have that coupon for the local gym?"

"I threw it into the trash last night," Sammi says. "Why?"

"I'm going to dig it out and join."

Michelle swallows her margarita. "What's wrong with the company gym?"

"Matt works out there."

Michelle and Sammi laugh, while I glare. They are not helping.

"You've done everything in your power to pick a man you'll never run into again, yet the universe is throwing him at you every chance it gets. So have you considered the possibility that maybe you should just screw him senseless and be done with it?" Sammi says.

"No. That's like giving up. Like when I was studying for the intermediate accounting final and kept falling asleep."

"I bet Matt can keep you up."

"And you can keep *him* up," Michelle adds.

I ignore the unhelpful commentary. "If I'd given in, I would've never graduated."

"I thought you did finance," Michelle says.

"Accounting's required."

"But this isn't a test." Sammi gestures with a chip. "It's just sex."

"'Lead me not into temptation...'."

Sammi waggles her beautifully arched eyebrows. "He's a *handsome* devil so he can tempt all he wants. Look, if you're seriously not interested, I'll take him."

My mouth opens. "What about your crush on David?" She's been infatuated with David since our first year at UVA.

"He's still unavailable, dating that worthless skank,

so what can I do?" She shrugs. "I'm not putting my sex life on hold until he's free."

"Hear, hear," Michelle says, banging on the table twice and downing the rest of her margarita.

"He meets all my requirements for boyfriend material until David's free." Sammi reaches for her phone and taps a few things. "He's single, played football in high school and at Notre Dame—"

"He played football?" That's news to me. David said they went to Harvard together. On the other hand, that explains the extra broad shoulders and ultra-sexy physique.

"Yeah. Quarterback. Hot, right? That's how he got that awesome bod. Anyway, he got injured his sophomore year, which ended his NFL aspirations, so he transferred to Harvard. Went there for both undergrad and law. Summa cum laude. He used to work for a huge-ass law firm in New York that specializes in defending corporate assholes, but he's seen the light so that can be forgiven. And he was truthful about being single and unattached since his Facebook profile says so."

"Are you Facebook friends with him?" I ask.

"Nah. Just got his public info."

Michelle frowns. "Have you been snooping around where you shouldn't?"

"Don't worry. I didn't touch the HR database."

Michelle makes a face. Sammi hacked into the database once to pull info on David. Thankfully, nobody noticed. The only reason why we know is that she fessed up one night while playing a drinking game during a *Mad Men* marathon.

"All this is public." Sammi leans closer. "Do you know he used to date Emma Beane?"

The name sounds familiar, but I can't place her. "Who's that?"

"A socialite. She married a shipping magnate from Greece five years ago. It's like a Harlequin romance— *The Hot Greek Tycoon's Pregnant Socialite Virgin.* Well, she probably wasn't one if she'd dated Matt before. Anyway they divorced a year ago."

It's my turn to get my phone out. I look up Emma Beane.

Google crushes me by showing me a photo of a beautiful, polished blonde with eyes as blue as the Mediterranean Sea, which, as it happens, is in the background. Her wavy hair blows around her. A strapless white dress fits her perfectly. It pushes her girls up for a bountiful cleavage, pinches her small waist and flows over gently flaring hips. Diamonds glitter at her ears and throat. She looks more like a Victoria's Secret model than a divorcée.

Holy shit gets stuck in my throat. That's the kind of woman Matt used to date?

If that's what he can get, why did he want to take me to bed on Friday?

I mean...I'm pretty enough. Nobody's complained about my green eyes or red hair, but I'm not model material. Not even close. I'm too short and too curvy. I glare at the half-full margarita glass. Drinking probably doesn't help, but a girl's gotta have some fun. Just not too much fun, because that makes her irresponsible.

Before I can feel even more pathetic and ridiculous, Diego shows up with our food. We dig in. Depressed or not, I'm hungry, and my belly won't be denied.

After I've wolfed down at least half my burrito, Sammi says, "Did you apply for the app dev team opening?"

I almost choke on my food. It's like Alexandra has taken over my best friend's mouth and is speaking through it. "What?"

"I saw it this morning and thought it was perfect for you. More fun than making David's coffee."

"Geez, thanks. Next time, I'm not telling you shit about what he's up to." I've been sort of helping Sammi keep track of David...because what else can you do when your best friend refuses to give up on your unavailable cousin?

"That's what Facebook and Instagram are for."

"You aren't his Facebook friend."

"I'm not an amateur. I created a fake account for that. Otherwise it wouldn't be stalking."

Michelle peers at her. "Do you want him to think you're stalking him?"

"Of course. Bet he'll be flattered I put in the effort." Sammi waves her fork around, a grilled onion drooping from the end. "Anyway, the point isn't about my stalking, but Jan's career." She turns to me. "I'm not having you screw up your career for my love life. It ain't worth it or right. Why do you think *I* never applied to be his assistant?"

"Because you're too good an app developer."

"So are you. I wouldn't have been able to make Bailey without you."

I snort. "Come on."

"*You* come on. I'm serious. You should go for it."

I eat the last bite and reach for my margarita. It's easy for her to say because she was one of the best engineering students at UVA, but not me. To this date, I don't understand how I got into the business program at Comm School.

Diego comes by to make sure we don't need anything else, and since I'm starting to crash after getting up an hour early, we ask for our check.

Suddenly, Sammi's brown eyes light up. "Incoming!"

"What?" I turn to see what she's looking at.

Jesus. *It's Matt.* And he's not alone.

He walks in with a stunning gray-eyed blonde. He's in the same pinstriped suit he wore at work, and the blonde is in a fitted sleeveless jade dress cinched with a thin yellow belt. Her thick, glossy hair is set in an artful French twist, secured with a gorgeous faux-diamond and pearl pin. She has a pair of diamond studs, and a platinum key pendant hangs from her neck. Her sky-high heels add at least four inches to her height, and she looks like a starlet. Hanging from her slim wrist is a black lambskin Lady Dior, a purse I've been admiring for ages without having the guts to splurge on one.

The hostess seats them at a rectangular table on the other side of the restaurant. I keep staring at her, cataloging our differences. I just came from the gym, am not wearing makeup, and my hair isn't exactly "stylish"...unless limp red spaghetti can be considered a style. She, on the other hand, is perfectly sophisticated and polished.

I bet she's never chickened out in the middle of sex. Or tried to brazen her way through an awkward meeting with an ex-romantic partner.

"He said he wasn't dating," I mutter, unspeakably peeved.

"Men. All liars," Michelle says with a small, apologetic shrug.

"The bastard should've updated his Facebook profile," Sammi grouses. "How are we supposed to keep up if he doesn't?"

I drain my glass, my eyes on Matt and his date. They're chatting, and he laughs at something she says. So she's super witty, too.

There's such an easy rapport and affection between them. Maybe he's found his soul mate between the gym and now. It can happen.

Or maybe they're related. *Right. They don't look anything like each other.*

As though he's sensed me, he turns his head, locks gazes.

Then he has the gall to smile.

Wait. That's not right. I don't have the right to be unhappy about this since we aren't an item. He doesn't even know he almost slept with me because he doesn't know I'm Bella from Brooklyn.

I give him a smile too.

"Bared teeth do not a smile make," Sammi says.

Just then Diego, that good man, brings our check. I give him an extra generous tip for the timing and we leave before Matt decides to do something crazy like introduce us to his date.

The drive back is a simmering exercise in not committing vehicular idiocy. As we park our cars and pile into the house, I declare, "Jan's Law is not going to prevail!"

"What's Jan's Law?" Michelle asks.

"The avalanche of crap I've been going through since Friday." I make a fist and wave it like Scarlett O'Hara in *Gone with the Wind*. "I'm going to do my job. He's going to get bored with Virginia and go back to Manhattan."

"Does this mean you aren't going to wear those glasses anymore?" Sammi asks.

I give her a look. "Of course I'm keeping the glasses. Let's not get too crazy here."

6

I toss for the hundredth time and hit one of the buttons on top of the digital alarm clock next to my bed. The screen lights up and lets me know it's almost one a.m.

I should've passed out the second my head hit the pillow. After all, I had an hour less sleep than normal, and I exercised. Normally that would be enough.

But my skin's too tight and prickly. And I'm achy between my legs.

Sighing, I stare at the dark ceiling. I may be a virgin, but I'm not ignorant. I know when I'm horny and want an orgasm. I haven't done anything to get myself off since leaving Matt's hotel room, and he did an excellent job of getting me hot and bothered today.

Maybe the undercurrent of sexual frustration is what's throwing me off. Men aren't the only ones with needs—let's not be sexist here—and my wants deserve as much TLC as anybody else's.

I reach into the drawer in my nightstand and pull out the vibrator I left there for occasions like this.

As the toy buzzes between my legs, I close my eyes and fantasize to help things along. I put myself back into that hotel room in New York...

Pulling me closer, he slanted his mouth over mine, dominating me, overwhelming my senses. His tongue swept inside, thrusting as though it had every right to be there, and I moaned softly at the way he took charge. I've never met a man who was so confident, so knowing. It was addictive and heady, and my blood grew hot in my veins.

He ran his hands all over my body, as though he couldn't wait to feel every smooth inch. Every time another piece of clothing came off, he groaned in approval. I've never felt more desirable than I did standing before him in nothing but my black lacy bra, the matching thong that's barely there, and strappy stiletto heels. He placed his mouth back on mine, cupped my breast as though he wanted to learn how it felt in his big callused hand, then trapped the nipple between two fingers through the lace and tugged until the sharp pleasure pulsed through me and ended in my pussy, leaving me wet and needy.

And only when I begged did he slip his clever, clever fingers under the tiny strip of my thong and toy with my swollen clit.

I let go of my breast and push my hand between my legs, roughly touching the opening of my pussy the way he did. *When the pad of his thumb bumped into my clit*

at the same time his finger pushed into me, I saw stars.
My back arches.

"God, you're so tight," he groaned against
my mouth.

He put a second finger in, stretching me impossibly,
and I rocked against him. Just like I'm rocking now
against my slimmer, softer hand and the vibrator.
*Although he was driving me faster and harder than any
man before him, I wasn't sure if that would be enough.
I'd never had a climax given to me by someone else.*

*But even if I didn't get off, I wouldn't be too upset
since everything else was perfect.*

*Maybe he sensed my uncertainty, but he kissed me
harder, his tongue thrusting into my mouth in sync with
his fingers pushing into my pussy. He curled the fingers,
making sure his thumb circled over my clit every time he
drove in. My breathing shallowed, and the pleasure
continued to peak and peak until even the soles of my
feet tingled.*

*When he pinched my nipple hard, the slight
pain/pleasure pushed me over the edge. I came,
screaming against his lips, shaking in his arms. He'd
gotten me off with just his fingers.*

And I pant as the vibrator gives me my orgasm, but
I'm not done. It was too soft, too anemic to really
satisfy. I turn up the speed as my mind wanders...

*I was greedy for more. I wanted—no, needed—to
know what he was like, how he would sound when he
came. Slowly, I rose to my knees, my eyes on his and my
palms against his sides, and pulled his cock into my*

mouth. He was so, so big and much thicker than the two fingers. My lips stretched tightly around the throbbing shaft. I loved the feel of the smooth, hard flesh inside me, and the way his salty precum slickened my tongue. The noise rumbling deep in his chest turned me on so fast, so hot, it was like I'd never even climaxed.

I used every trick I'd learned from reading about sex and watching porn. Lightly scratching his scrotum, cupping and stimulating his balls, then brushing my fingertip over the tight rosette of his anus, pushing very lightly against it when he groaned in approval.

"I'm going to come," he warned, his voice guttural.

I didn't let him go. Instead I tightened my grip on him and sucked even harder. I wanted him to feel as good as he made me feel, and I was drunk on his pleasure and mine.

I cover my mouth as a second orgasm ripples through me, moaning into my palm. I pant softly in my empty bedroom. It's satisfying, although not as good as the one he gave me with his fingers.

With a groan, I turn off the vibrator, roll over and bury my face in the pillow. Damn it, damn it, damn it! I just got myself off fantasizing about what Matt and I did on Friday.

7

By the time Saturday rolls around, I almost feel silly about being so freaked out over Matt moving in next door and working at Sweet Darlings. He hasn't come by David's office since Monday, and we haven't run into each other at work or around the neighborhood. Since I joined the local gym, we have no contact after work either.

Still, I'd be lying if I said I don't think about him and the blonde...or that it doesn't bother me...because it does, no matter how irrational my reaction is about the whole thing.

I even stopped masturbating since Monday night. I just can't avail myself of B.O.B. until I can be certain that I won't be thinking of Matt. Instead of waiting for the business trip next year, I should just fly to Vegas or something and get laid. Sixth time's gotta be the charm, right? I mean, it has twice the power of the third time.

Around ten, I drive to Alexandra's house for the

birthday party. I already got the gift she wanted—a charitable contribution in her name. I selected an organization that specializes in helping new mothers and their babies. Given that so many of Sweet Darlings Inc.'s customer base are new parents, it seems fitting.

Although I arrive a little early, the driveway is already packed with fancy cars. My Altima is easily the humblest among the bunch, and I prefer it that way. It seems pretentious to drive a flashy car, especially on my assistant's salary. When I make more or get promoted, I'll upgrade...maybe.

Alexandra's house is a sprawling two-story structure that occupies a half-acre lot. She has a huge garden, although she doesn't do much gardening now. I can hear music and voices coming from the backyard.

"Hey, there you are!" David says with a huge grin. He's dressed casually in a T-shirt and shorts. "Come on over."

"I thought the party didn't start until eleven."

"Yeah, but Mom wanted to cook brunch for Grandma."

"It must've been something awesome." David's mother—Aunt Sun, to me—is equal parts Chinese, Korean, French and Italian, and she cooks better than most professional chefs working at fancy restaurants.

"There's still some French toast if you want."

"Wow. Who didn't show?"

He laughs. "She just made too much."

When we walk into the big, open kitchen together, Aunt Sun is putting away some pots. With her hair glossy jet black and skin smooth, she doesn't look a day over thirty-five, although she has three children, all of them in their mid- to late twenties. She's dressed in a cute pink knit top, cropped denim pants and flats. Her brown almond-shaped eyes are warm as she waves at me. "Come, child. Pull up a chair." She serves a thick piece of French toast and smothers it with maple syrup, topping the whole thing off with fresh berries. She knows exactly how I like mine.

"You look fantastic," she says. "Have you lost weight? Here, you should eat this. Have to keep your strength up."

I nod, my lips twitching. Aunt Sun is always torn between two conflicting desires—to see her charges look fashionably slim and to feed them all the culinary delights she can whip up. Since she doesn't believe in using low-calorie substitutes for any ingredients, she has to know eating as much as she wants us to would widen everyone in the family enough to sink the Titanic.

My cousins move back and forth in the house like three separate schools of fish. Everyone's dressed casually—that's how Alexandra wanted it. But that doesn't mean they look any less polished. The Darlings know how to shine like pearls no matter what. Sort of like Matt's ex and his current flavor of blonde.

I'd like to think I'm a Darling too, shining like a pearl, but I know better. I'm the proverbial red-headed stepchild—literally. I can't decide if I'm different from my cousins because of who my dad is. I'm never going to find out who or what kind of man he is. For all I know, he could be sitting in jail or...orbiting our planet, rocking in style. I wish Mom had had better judgment, but if she had, she wouldn't have run with him, would she? Then I would've never been born, so all these questions are moot. I sigh. As families go, I lucked out overall. The Darlings are nice people, and it's not their fault I'm never going to be as graceful, elegant or smart as they are.

And that's about as deep as I'm going because I'm not about to get depressed about my life when it's a pretty good one by anybody's standards. I should be grateful. I *am* grateful.

"Want some mimosa, dear?" asks Aunt Margo. She's the mother of Kathleen, Alec and Cora. And she's absolutely stunning. Kathleen and Cora had to get their runway model looks from somewhere.

I nod. "Sure."

She hands me a full glass. She was always one of the coolest adults I knew growing up. Unlike most of the parental units, she was pretty loose with rules, including alcohol. Her motto was she'd rather have her children be bad when she was around to keep an eye on things than behind her back when she wasn't. Prohibition couldn't stop people from drinking, and no age restriction will stop kids if they really want something.

And it worked. When we got to college, none of us were really that hyped up about partying for the sake of free booze or binge drinking. Alcohol just didn't represent the allure of freedom and adulthood.

Our favorite DJ sets up his station and starts the music. This family doesn't party without good music, and Alexandra has excellent taste. Uncles Jimmy, George, Dan and Eddie start the giant grills in the back because none of them is willing to give up control of the barbecue to anyone else. They may cooperate in the boardroom, but cookouts are another matter entirely.

Grandmother comes in from the back and hugs me. "So glad you could come, dear. I wasn't sure. David told me you seemed a bit...tense this week. Are you well?"

My cousin and his big mouth. "I'm fine."

"I heard you haven't been to the gym the entire week either."

See? Told you. "Actually, I joined a local gym. They have this kickboxing class I wanted to take."

"Really? I didn't know kickboxing was so popular."

"The instructor is Thai, I think. I'm sure it's pretty authentic." That's such a lie. I have no idea where he's from. But he could be Thai, and my grandmother doesn't need to know the real reason I joined the gym.

"I'm sure it's working fabulously for her," Aunt Sun says. "Just look at how much more toned she looks."

Thank you. A glowing golden halo appears around her head, and I'm definitely getting her whatever she wants for Christmas. A family friend's arrival distracts Grandma, and I breathe softly with relief and finish my mimosa.

At eleven thirty the party starts with the cake—a giant, triple-tiered Wonder Woman-themed piece of art —lit with sixty-five candles. Alexandra extinguishes them all in two attempts. You gotta give her props for lung capacity. Must be all that working out.

Once that's out of the way, it's all about eating, drinking and dancing. No party of Alexandra's is complete without dancing, and she leads the conga line as usual.

The other family members join. They're all superb dancers. But then they all had at least five years of lessons.

"Come on, Jan," Cora gestures, swaying her body to the upbeat tune.

I shake my head. "I'm digesting my food."

There's no way I'm going out there and humiliating myself. I'm probably the only person in the world to fall flat on her face during her first ballet lesson. Or trip and skin a knee trying to tango. At some point I gotta accept I'm just not like everyone else in the family. I'm the only one who didn't go to an Ivy League school (and the fact that I got accepted into a top-tier university at all shocked the hell out of Alexandra, who for once literally became slack-jawed and speechless when I told her). I'm the only one who can't ski, or swim (although I can float)...or play any musical instrument... or sing or dance. And none of it was because Alexandra skimped on lessons. She got me the best coaches and teachers, but you know...I'm just not that talented, not like the others are. A small sliver of me might always wonder if things could've been different if I hadn't been dumped onto them like an unwanted but unre-jectable package when I was ten. What would my life have been like if I'd had the warmth and confidence and closeness extended family can provide from the moment I was born?

Aunt Sun reaches for my hand. "Dancing helps with digestion."

I step away. "Sorry, nature calls."

Before anybody can say something like, "Hey, come join us as soon as you're done," I make my way to the second floor and slip inside Alexandra's empty study. I only need to give myself half an hour or so; the dancing will sort of die down as people take little breaks, and I won't be asked to make an idiot of myself.

The door opens, and I stiffen. It better not be one of my cousins trying to drag me downstairs.

My mouth ready to fire off some smart retort, I spin around. Whatever I was about to say vanishes. Because the person who just walked through the door? It's not one of my cousins. It's Matt. My One-Night Stand Number Five.

8

I stare. *How can Matt be here?* And how can he look so damn good in just a simple white shirt and jeans? The shirt clings to his muscled chest and flat, hard stomach. My gutter mind thinks back on what happened last time we were alone in that room... and how I came twice just reminiscing about it. I run my tongue over my lower lip before I catch myself.

His mouth quirks. "So this is where you're going to hide."

"I'm not *hiding*. I have a headache." Not really, but close enough.

He steps forward until we're only a foot apart. I can feel the heat radiating from his big body and swallow.

"Is that why you left?" he asks.

"Why else—"

"Bella."

Every part, every atom of me freezes. A beat later, I croak out, "What?"

"Bella. Jan. Does it matter?"

"You know...?"

"How could I not?" He comes even closer and cradles my face in his big hands.

A breath shudders out of me, and I shiver. The skin where he touches is searing, and it feels a hundred times better than the memory. "Matt... Um..." I have no idea what I'm going to say. I mean...what *do* you say in a situation like this?

"I'm going to kiss you, Jan." He tilts my head, his dipping lower until our breaths mingle. "If you want me to stop, tell me now."

Heat unfurls inside my belly. My heart beats once. Twice.

But before his mouth descends over mine, I blurt out, "Wait! What about your date?"

He stops. "My *what*?"

"The blonde at the restaurant." Taking advantage of his momentary shock, I pull away.

He blinks. Gives me an "I honestly have no idea what you're talking about" look.

Oh no. I'm not falling for that. I may not have Michelle's cynicism, but I'm not a complete idiot. "Don't try to deny it. I saw you on Monday at Carlos's." I cross my arms. "You guys looked *extra* chummy." And she's really beautiful, unjustly so.

His lips twitch, then he throws his head back and laughs. "Sweet Jesus, that was my sister."

"You guys looked nothing alike. I checked." Oops. I press my lips together. Now I sound like a jealous, deranged one-night stand abortée.

"Yeah, because I'm a carbon copy of my dad, and she took after our maternal grandmother." He wipes tears at his eyes. "Oh man, wait until I tell her."

"Don't you dare!" I blurt out. It seems a bit unreal that the blonde is his sister, but there's no way he can be faking his hilarity. Or else he's in the wrong field.

He sobers, although his eyes are still bright with amusement. "I see that you aren't saying no."

No...? Oh. A bolt of excitement jolts through me. The kiss. My jaw tilts slightly as though in permission.

And that's all I needed to do.

He pulls me close, his hand at the small of my back, a palm cupping my cheek. His mouth descends over mine. I brace myself. I don't say no—I can't, and I don't know what kind of kiss I'm going to get from him after getting busted for giving him a fake name, sneaking around and avoiding him, and now the ridiculous thing over his sister.

But his lips are lush over mine, tender and exploratory. I shake with relief and heat, kissing him back. I part my mouth and let my tongue glide across his. He tastes better than I remember with a hint of wine, lust and all him.

He tunnels a hand into my unbound hair and tugs. The slight pain heightens my pleasure, and I'm slick between my legs, my muscles tense in anticipation.

"I don't know how you thought I wouldn't recognize you," he murmurs against my swollen lips. "Your scent, your eyes, your voice—everything about you is the same and turns me on like nothing else." He nuzzles my neck. "Besides, I could never forget you when you owe me something."

It's hard to process what he's saying when he's running his mouth along the sensitive skin over my collarbone. His hot breaths fan against me, sending sweet shivers down my spine.

"I gave you a blow job," I manage. I'd never felt the urge to give one to anyone, but with him, I felt an overwhelming need to do it, especially after the lovely orgasm he gave me.

"My dear Jan, a blow job is not what all men want from their lovers."

I stiffen, the pleasurable haze dissipating. "I'm not having intercourse with you." I'm on the pill, but I don't have a condom on me. I supply my own—making sure they're not expired or tampered with. I know it's paranoid, but I can't help myself. Anything less and I can't really let myself go. Not that I've exactly been able to let go thus far, given that my hymen is still intact.

He nips my earlobe. "That's not what I was talking about."

I relax slightly. "Then?" I whisper, trying hard to focus, which is impossible with his mouth on me.

"When you were on your knees, looking gorgeous with your pink cheeks hollowed, lips tight around my cock...and when you pulled me harder and deeper into you when I said I was about to come... Do you have any idea how much I wanted to spread you open and eat you out? Make you come until you couldn't even remember your own name?"

I exhale softly at the scorching picture he's drawing with his words. My panties are totally soaked through. I bite my lower lip, but a needy whimper rises anyway. My face heats as his searing blue gaze bores into mine.

"I'm going to do exactly that right now," he says, his voice deeper and guttural with lust.

"There are people downstairs." It doesn't quite come out like a protest the way I expected it to. Instead it sounds like I'm pointing out an obstacle he ought to take care of before we begin, so we can avoid cunnilingus interruptus.

"I locked the door when I came in, and you'll just have to be quiet. But not too quiet...I want to hear you." He tilts my head for another kiss, this time more dominating and masterful.

I cling to him, heat rolling through me. I've never really cared for men going down on me. Most of the time it feels perfunctory, like they're doing it so they can stick their dick inside a little bit later, or—worse— it's a chore to be performed so they don't appear lousy in bed.

But with Matt, I know it will be different. It's going to be toe-curling, just like all those romance novels I read, because a man doesn't pursue a woman for that unless he loves it and genuinely wants to do it.

His hand closes around my breast, and I moan. He seems to know exactly how much to squeeze, how I want my nipple played with. His thumb feels amazing through my shirt and bra, and I arch into his touch.

He caresses the taut skin on my thigh and puts a hand on my hip. Unbearably aroused, I rock against him, cradling his thick, throbbing erection against my body and loving it. He laughs, the wicked sound inflaming my nerve endings. I ache deep inside. It's so intense, it's almost painful.

"Please, Matt," I whisper. "Please, please, please."

His eyes grow darker, and he shoves my pants and panties out of the way. I kick them off, not caring where they land. All that matters is him—and me—and this crazy heat between us.

He pushes me backward until my bare butt's propped against the huge desk. I brace myself on my palms, so I can watch what he's doing.

Placing his hands on my knees, he spreads them as wide as he can, then groans. "Look at you. So pretty, so juicy."

The frank admiration in his gaze burns away my embarrassment. My ragged breathing sounds so loud in the room.

He dips his fingers between my slick folds, then pulls out and licks them clean. "So tasty. To think I almost didn't take you with me that night..."

"Why not?"

"You look like the kind of girl I should call the next morning."

My pleasure-slugged mind shivers with a warning, not that I can grasp what I should worry about. He took me to his hotel that night. We had fun, until I bailed. And we're about to have fun again...right?

Still... A tiny sliver of sanity tells me to take a step back. But its voice is snuffed when Matt positions his head between my legs, spreads me with his fingers and licks me with the flat of his tongue as though I were the sweetest ice cream.

The touch is electrifying. White-hot bliss streaks from my core all the way to my fingertips and toes.

My head falls back, a moan building deep in my throat. He devours me with everything he has, his lips, tongue and just the tiniest bit of teeth to add a hint of pain that only serves to heighten my senses. He wasn't just talking when he said he'd eat me out.

Lush pleasure blooms within me, and I'm already so, so close. My chest rises and falls in rapid, uneven staccato beats.

He sucks my clit hard into his mouth while pushing two thick fingers into me. I cry out softly at the sudden invasion, then I'm lost as he curls them and bumps into the über-sensitive spot inside me. I move my hips, grinding like a shameless hussy against his face. Soft, desperate words fall from my lips—*please, please, yes, more, Matt, oh God.*

A forceful orgasm ravages me, and I can tell I'm going to be hoarse from the silent scream lodged in my throat. My lungs are heaving, but Matt's not finished as he spreads me wider, more vulnerable. He adds another finger and pushes as deep as he can. It feels unbelievable to be stretched to the limit, to experience the relentless throbbing and need coursing through my veins. He's the one on his knees between my legs, but it's me who's at his mercy.

He wrings another mind-shattering orgasm out of me. My body isn't mine to control, back arching, toes curling and my whole frame shaking...then turning to a boneless heap on the desk.

"Beautiful," he murmurs between soft kisses on my thighs. "So sweet."

I bring him up and lick his mouth. He tastes like himself—and me. It's erotic and surprisingly intimate.

He reaches into his back pocket and pulls out a plain, white handkerchief, which he uses to wipe between my legs. It's a little embarrassing and even a bit awkward, which is silly given how I ground myself against his face. But as embarrassing as my out-of-control behavior was, I can't be too mortified... What was I *supposed* to do? Perch there like a proper lady? But right now is a bit different. Besides, he's still hard. It's impossible to miss the thickness pressing against his pants, and I wonder if I should do something about it, although I'm not sure exactly what since I already told him no intercourse. Maybe offer him a hand job? But isn't it awkward just to blurt it out? Why isn't he signaling what he wants instead of cleaning me up?

To hide my discomfiture, I raise my eyebrows and say, "Were you a Boy Scout? You, um, come prepared."

"Yes, but even if I weren't an Eagle Scout—which I am—I still would've brought this along." He gives me a wink. "I knew I'd run into you at today's party."

"How'd you get invited? It's for family and friends only."

"David."

I sigh. *Of course.* I can't decide if I should hug my cousin or kill him. Maybe both. "Does he know about... you know..." I flick my wrist back and forth between him and me.

"No. I don't lick"—Matt brushes his lips over my neck—"and tell."

"Oh." I clear my throat. "Good."

He pockets the handkerchief and picks up my red lace bikini and pants. He hands me the pants, but not the underwear.

I take the pants, then say, "I need my underwear."

"You aren't seriously telling me you're going to put wet panties back on?"

My face flames. This is awkward. I'm not in control of the venue or the situation, which is new to me. I don't even have Bailey to help me. "Of course not, but they're mine."

"Want them back?" He grins, flashing me that cute dimple that I found irresistibly adorable when we first met. "Have dinner with me."

"Get real." I pull on my pants since arguing with my lady parts hanging out puts me at a considerable disadvantage, especially when the other guy is a lawyer.

"I mean it. Dinner. Tonight. You can have your panties back then. I'll even have them laundered, dried and pressed."

I laugh. "No way. No dinner. You can keep them."

He sticks a finger into one of the holes and starts twirling the scrap of red lace. It looks positively obscene. "You sure? It's an awfully sexy pair."

"Stop doing that. They're not a toy."

"More like a wrapper for me to rip off you."

I flush, hating that I'm so lightly complexioned. "That's one of my favorite pairs, but you can keep them. I'll just buy another."

"What's it going to take?"

I play dumb. "I don't know, but probably less than twenty."

"Jan." His voice takes on an edge. "You're a smart woman."

I huff. "I don't date."

"Really? You just put out?"

"Yup. Sex without all the dating stuff." I don't mention my V-Card or Baileying over and over because they both sound sort of foolish and immature, even though I can't help either of them. I should really just forget looking for One-Night Stand Number Six and see a therapist who can delve into the deepest recesses of my mind and tell me what's down there.

"You should—at a minimum—get great meals, movies and flowers out of the deal. That's the least you deserve."

"Why?" I ask, genuinely curious. I mean, he could just latch on to the sex part. Dating means sticking around. Expectations. Complications.

"Supply and demand."

I snort. "You sound like David in marketing meetings."

"No. I sound like a lawyer negotiating."

I cant my head and study him. "Then you're doing a crummy job."

He flicks the tip of my nose with his finger. "I'm negotiating on your behalf."

"Against yourself?"

"It's not a 'you win, I lose' or 'I win, you lose' scenario. It's called mutual benefit."

"Sounds to me like a euphemism for self-dealing."

He laughs softly. "Sweetheart, you don't want me on the other side of a negotiating table."

Him calling me sweetheart with half-amusement, half-affection sends lovely shivers along my spine, but I'm not ready to give in or deviate from my plan. "We have a non-fraternization policy at work." And if we don't, we should, *starting now*, given how much Alexandra seems to disapprove of—

"No, we don't." He smirks. "I already checked."

"Maybe you missed it."

"I'm a lawyer. I don't miss things."

Hmm. A Harvard summa cum laude probably *doesn't* miss anything. I make a snap decision. "Fine. We can have dinner. But no intercourse." I raise a finger before he can interrupt me. "If we do it your way on the dating part, I get to say no intercourse."

He gives me a triumphant smile. And that throws me off. Shouldn't he get huffy and pouty?

"Unexpected, but then I wouldn't have found you

fascinating if you were predictable. Deal." He dips his head and kisses me, just a fleeting brush of his lips against mine, yet I feel it all the way to the tips of my toes. "Nothing but a steady diet of oral can get old, but I have a feeling it can be kept fresh and interesting with you."

I sputter. "What?"

"Didn't you know? Oral doesn't count as intercourse." He winks. "I'll pick you up at seven."

9

Sammi looks up from her laptop the moment I walk through the door. "How was the party?"

"I have a date," I wail. "And I only have two hours to get ready! Is Michelle home?" She's the only one to talk to for stuff like what I'm going to wear.

"Yeah." Sammi points toward the ceiling. "But with who? How? Did one of your cousins set you up?"

Ignoring her, I go upstairs. She follows, firing more questions. She really should've been a CIA interrogator. Or if it ever becomes possible, travel back in time and become a Spanish Inquisidor. (Or would that be Inquisidora, since she's a woman...?)

I find Michelle in the bathroom, a lock of brown hair in a curling iron. She smiles. "Hey. So who's the lucky guy?" she asks, apparently having heard Sammi's questions.

"Matt."

Sammi gasps. "You mean the Dick replacement?"

"I thought you hadn't seen him since Monday," Michelle says.

"He was at Alexandra's party," I say.

Michelle nods. "He cornered you, didn't he?"

"In a manner of speaking." I'm not going into more detail than that.

"That's hot. A man who doesn't give up easily." Michelle finishes curling her hair. "Give the guy a chance. How bad can it be?"

Sammi adopts her wise woman expression. "Exactly. Plans change. One-night stands can be nice, but never discount advantages of a steady boyfriend, especially one as sexy as ThaYuMNDo."

"Meals, movies, flowers," I repeat Matt's list.

"Chocolate," Michelle says.

Chocolate! Matt completely forgot that one, but I'll remind him later. "My problem is, what do I wear?"

"Something slutty, of course," Sammi says.

I roll my eyes. "I'm not prowling to pick up my next one-night stand."

"Where is he taking you?" Michelle asks.

"He didn't say. And I forgot to ask."

"How could you forget something that important?"

I shrug, my face extra warm. I'm not getting into the whole thing about whether or not oral sex counts as intercourse, which distracted me no end.

"Call him," Michelle says.

"Can't. I don't know his number. His car isn't outside either," I add, in case Sammi tells me to go over.

"I have his digits." Sammi rattles off a New York number.

"How did you get that? Never mind." Better I don't know. That way I can't be forced to testify against her.

Michelle walks through my room to my walk-in closet. Her feet spread shoulder width apart, she studies what I have, one hand on her chin. "How about this?" She points at a cream-colored sheath dress. "Classy and flattering. Perfect for a first date."

When I look at it skeptically, she pulls it out and puts it in front of me. "There. It's so you."

Sammi nods. "Have to agree. And now that we've settled on a dress, I really want to know how he managed to snag you for a date." Then she suddenly snaps her fingers. "Speaking of which, you need to stop by the store and buy a fresh box of condoms. He looks like he has some serious stamina."

Based on the temperature of my cheeks, my face must be beet red. "There's no need. He knows it won't lead to anything."

Sammi and Michelle both go still and stare at me. Sammi is the first to break the silence. "What do you mean?"

"I told him no sex." Technically no intercourse, but my housemates don't need to know that. Or how Matt reacted to my dictate. I still don't know why I used the term *intercourse* rather than *sex*. It's like my dirty, dirty mind suddenly wrested control of my mouth from my brain.

"I think he likes you," Sammi singsongs, giving me a sly look.

"No, he doesn't. We don't know each other well enough for that."

"A guy has to like the girl a lot if he's going to date her without any expectation of sex," she says.

"Or he has a sneaky move planned." Michelle looks worried. "Watch your food and drinks."

I gape at her. "He's a coworker. And an *upstanding* lawyer. The company wouldn't have hired him otherwise."

"No, you have it all wrong. He's a *damn good* lawyer, which is why he was hired. Which also means he knows all the ways he can weasel out of criminal charges."

"Is that how you look at your mother's work?"

"She only handles divorce." Michelle shrugs. "Says they're more dramatic and interesting than criminal proceedings. Anyway, I need to go. The world's full of cheaters, and I *gotta catch 'em all.*" She sings the last part and stops by her room to pick up her purse. "Ciao! Do everything I wouldn't do tonight with your Matt!"

I shake my head. Michelle tempts men without putting out. "He's not mine," I call to her vanishing back.

Sammi chuckles, then goes to her room. "FYI, I'm gonna be out all night if you want to bring Matt home," she calls out while typing something on her computer.

"Where are you going?"

"Meeting a few friends then stopping at my

parents' for a nightcap. I'm sure Mom's going to insist that I sleep over."

"But you never say yes to that." Sammi loves her parents, but she doesn't like to be smothered, or so she says. I don't understand it, but then I've never felt what she considers "smothering" parental love. I wish I had.

"Today's special. I'm legit trying to make you happy."

"You know Matt lives right next door."

"Uh-huh, but it's time your bed sees some action."

"Get your mind out of the gutter."

"Why? It's comfortable down here."

I laugh, but then sober a bit and sit on the edge of her messy bed. "I don't know, Sammi. I feel like I should cancel."

"What's really going on?" She props her chin on a hand. "Come on. Talk to me."

"What if... I mean, dates are awkward, and I've always ended up not liking the guy afterward."

"You've actually dated?"

I roll my eyes. "Just because I'm a virgin doesn't mean I've never gone out."

"Oh yeah. That's right. Those boys you had dinner with, then came home early, all grumpy." Sammi nods. "Okay, here's what I think. If you end up not liking Matt after this, who cares?" She shrugs. "You didn't want to like the guy or do anything further with him last week when you found out he moved in next door. So I'd say it's a great opportunity."

Put that way, it makes perfect sense, except I don't

want that. I don't want to not like Matt. It's ridiculously perverse, but I want the man who starred in my fantasy to remain a nice guy even if he really isn't. Maybe that's why Mom ran away with Dad and never came back to the family. Maybe she didn't want to admit she was wrong about what kind of man Dad was.

"You're overanalyzing this," Sammi says, her voice surprisingly gentle. "Just don't think about anything and have fun with him. He may surprise you. You never know."

In the end I put on a hot pink scoop-neck shirt and dove gray denim pants, paired with casual beige sandals. The dress Michelle picked out is pretty, but somehow it feels wrong for the evening. Sammi left an hour ago, so I pamper myself in the massage chair, set to stop exactly at seven.

The moment the chair stills, I hear two strong knocks. I hop off and open the door.

Matt fills the doorframe, his big body loose and relaxed. He's in a blue V-neck shirt and gray slacks that mold to narrow hips and show hints of the muscled legs underneath. Even when he's dressed casually, it's obvious he has great taste and money from the way his clothes fit him. He walks inside, closing the door. He offers me a bouquet with a sunflower in the middle, then kisses me softly.

"Unusual," I remark, trying to hide how absurdly

pleased I am, although I'm certain my flush is betraying me. Damn my complexion!

"But just what you like." He grins.

"Yes." I adore sunflowers. They're so cheery, and when I have one in my room, I feel like I have a miniature sun right there to brighten my day. "Let me put these in some water."

An upper kitchen cabinet has several vases, gifts from Alexandra and Michelle's mom. I find a sizable crystal one, fill it with water and put the bouquet in. This baby's definitely going into my bedroom after I come back.

Matt waits for me to finish, then hands me another gift in a small, glossy paper bag in pink.

"What is it?" I say, moving the tissue paper around to see what's inside.

"Your panties."

I raise an eyebrow. "I told you you didn't have to."

"And I said I would."

I don't have to check to know they're laundered and pressed. This man takes his commitments seriously, no matter how casual the circumstances. Most guys I know would've forgotten...or tried to keep them as a trophy.

I put the bag on the floor by the massage chair. "So where are we going?"

"You'll see." He smiles winsomely.

I tilt my head, then decide it doesn't matter. Based on his outfit, what I have on is fine for whatever restaurant we're going to.

As I sling my purse over a shoulder, he takes my free hand. My heart skips a beat. It's innocent and natural, like we're meant to have our fingers linked.

I'm being ridiculous. I shake myself mentally. Can he feel my slightly unsteady pulse through the contact, which feels more intimate than it should? This is what comes from inexperience. There's no other explanation for my absurd reaction. I mean, we've gotten a lot more personal than this already.

To my surprise, he doesn't lead me to the BMW in his driveway. Instead he takes me to his house. He opens the door and gestures gallantly.

I hesitate. "Uh... Your housemate hasn't come back, right?" ThaMaNDo's car isn't outside, but you never know.

"Housemate?"

"You know... The guy who moved in before you did?"

"You mean Uncle Bob?"

My jaw drops. "Uncle? That was your uncle?"

Matt nods. "Yeah. On my mother's side."

Oh geez. That man—Bob—looks nothing like Matt...or his sister.

"And to answer your question, he's not here. He lives in Arlington. He was helping me with my relocation."

"Were you adopted?" I blurt out, unable to help myself.

"What?" He laughs as he gently directs me inside.

I step into a bright foyer with a high ceiling, then

turn to face him. "You look nothing like your sister or your uncle..." I clear my throat, then lower my voice. "You don't have any strange habits, do you?"

He gives me a look. "Like what?"

"Like...um...dancing?" Not that I would mind terribly if Matt decided to dance naked, but I'm not sure how I feel about every woman in the neighborhood watching through the window.

Matt covers his eyes with a hand. "Oh no. He didn't... Did he?"

"He did. Numerous times."

He shakes his head. "Sorry about that. He can be a little...unique from time to time. We've been telling him not to do things that can scar his neighbors for life, but it doesn't seem to stick any better than LSAT prep."

"Did he try to be a lawyer?"

Matt nods. "Like everyone else in the family. But he still doesn't know what perjury is."

"Wow." As interesting as solving the mystery of who ThaMaNDo is, what really catches my attention is the whole deal about Matt's family being lawyers. If Matt and my short glimpse of his sister are anything to go by, all of them, except Bob, must be superbly accomplished.

He goes to the kitchen to check something that sounds like it's bubbling. Now that I'm no longer worried about spending time with a guy who likes to jiggle his naked body, I notice how amazing whatever's on the stove smells. It has a hint of garlic, tomatoes, herbs and meat, and it takes me back to my early childhood, when Mom used to make me my favorite pasta.

While Matt's busy, I check out the house. It's laid out similarly to my place, but decorated much more sparsely, although no less comfortably. His coffee table is hewn oak, and black remotes lie on the right edge. A big sectional couch faces the huge TV. A thick rug covers the sizable space between a fireplace and a couple of Barcaloungers, and there are framed pieces of contemporary art on the cream-colored walls. Unlike his uncle, he has the curtains drawn in the living room.

"Cream and sage lace, huh?" I say with a grin.

Matt groans from the kitchen. "Mom's house-warming gift. So..." He sighs. "Should've bought curtains before she sent me those, so I could've sent them back."

"I think it's sweet."

"Oh, there's nothing sweet about the gift."

I tilt my head. Did he ask for something else, but she insisted on sending those instead? Still, it was thoughtful, no?

"Anyway, you can pick whatever music you want," he says quickly, as though he doesn't want to talk about his mother anymore.

So I return to the island in the kitchen to take the tablet from him. His taste is eclectic: rock to modern pop to classical. I settle on a collection of Debussy because Grandma said you can never go wrong with him, especially when you aren't sure.

"What's for dinner?" I ask.

"Spaghetti with meatballs, garlic toast and salad. Three different flavors of ice cream. Oh, and we have chocolate."

My lips twitch. "Do you now?"

"Uh-huh. Why?"

"Nothing." I shake my head. And we thought he'd forgotten chocolate earlier. The man overlooks nothing.

"Since neither of us are going to be driving, we can drink anything in the house."

"Let me see." I check out his alcohol collection. He has a wine cooler plus a huge liquor cabinet, both stuffed with excellent bottles. Then I spot margarita mix stuck in the back of the cooler. "How about this?" I say, pulling it out. "And you just happen to have a bottle of tequila."

He grins. "An excellent choice. I forgot I had that." He takes out the tequila.

I take a stool at the island, rest an elbow on the smooth marble top and prop my chin. I watch him spike the mix with a generous serving of tequila. "You knew, didn't you?"

"I did my homework."

"So when you were lying low the past four days..."

"I was strategizing. I wasn't going to go in blind and mess it up. It was obvious you didn't want to see me anymore, and I had to find where the crack in the wall was."

"My walls don't have cracks."

"Every wall has at least one." He gives me a glass

and our fingers brush, sending a small tingle down my arm.

I take it with a murmured thanks and take a sip. It's excellent, with a smooth subtle heat from the tequila. *Mmmm.* I approve. "It was nothing personal," I clarify, just in case.

"I didn't think it was." He pours himself a big serving of the margarita.

"It was... It was supposed to be an out-of-town fling. I thought it'd be awkward to run into each other again, especially at work," I explain. He doesn't call me on the lameness of the explanation, so I think he understands. I hope.

He serves dinner. Meatballs smothered in tomato sauce topped with melted provolone cheese is one of my favorites and my number one comfort food. Mom used to make the dish for me when I was a kid, and I still have an absurdly soft spot for it even though I don't go out of my way to eat it.

I take an eager bite. Matt's version is perfect, with the pasta cooked al dente and sauce and meatballs flavorful. "This is good."

"I'm glad." He smiles softly. "My great grandmother's recipe."

"Really?"

"Why the surprise?"

"I thought maybe you bought this from a restaurant or something. How do you have the time to master everything?"

"When I decide to do something, I just make time."

"And manage to do everything well."

He merely grins.

I polish off my meal, then sit back with another margarita. The whole evening's nice. No, *nice* isn't quite right. The word is *lovely*. The food is homey and excellent, the drinks are delicious and the company's awesome. Even if we hadn't had a little sexy time in Alexandra's house, I'd know Matt was attracted to me—it's in his dark gaze, the soft gentle brush of his hands against me, all of it seemingly innocent but sending sparks of excitement to my heart. But he doesn't behave as though I have eyes on my breasts or that I'm supposed to put out now that he's fed me. He also doesn't try to show off how smart and clever he is, unlike some of the obnoxious Ivy League bores I've had the misfortune to run into, or ply me with empty compliments in a thinly veiled attempt to get me naked.

He just chats, sharing ordinary things that seem more interesting (to me at least) because they're about him. His childhood, his favorite food, the crazy antics of his sister, who he obviously loves. But he also makes sure to draw tidbits out from my side, too, without sounding like he's interrogating me. And I talk about my childhood a little, something I haven't done with other guys, and bring up some funny things that happened to me, too.

Maybe this is what's been missing before. I can't remember a time I've been totally, utterly relaxed and happy with a guy I was thinking about sleeping with. Not only that, I'm starting to like Matt.

He puts away our empty plates, taps his tablet a few times, and brings out a platter of dark chocolates—my favorite. The music changes to something sweet and sultry. My heart throbs to the beat.

I finish my fourth margarita and put a square of chocolate in my mouth. It melts like rich, cocoa-flavored butter. He takes a bite of the dessert, then stands and pulls me up from the couch. "Dance with me."

"I shouldn't. You're going to end up with a broken toe...or worse."

He chuckles. "You can't be that bad."

"Oh yes, I can. Why did you think I didn't dance at Alexandra's party?"

"C'mon. I promise not to sue."

I laugh. "Is that how lawyers pick up women? I won't sue if anything goes wrong?"

"Yes. And it usually works." He draws me to the empty space in the living room, and wraps me in his arms. I let him because even though I'm protesting about the dance, I like the feel of his hands on my bare skin. And the hot, dark way he drinks me in. Oh, and let's not forget his thick erection pushing against me. That's super exciting.

"I'm really clumsy," I say. "You heard the disclaimer, so don't say you didn't."

"You probably just had bad teachers. Didn't you say I manage to do everything well?"

"Do you teach people how to dance too? I have the coordination of a drunken two-year-old."

"Uh-huh. Why don't you let me be the judge?"

He pulls me a little tighter against his hard body. I feel electric sparks everywhere we touch, even through our clothes. My mouth dries, and my tongue feels thick and clumsy, and I can't say no.

"Just follow my lead."

I nod.

And we're dancing. He is—as I expected—a great dancer. He knows exactly how to move, how to lead. Of course I'm as terrible as always, messing up more than once. But he doesn't react in any way except to run a soothing hand along my back, which tenses every time I screw up, until I relax again.

I lay my head in the crook where his shoulder meets his chest. His body heat seems to turn my muscles to pliant goo, and he smells so sexy, all Matt underneath that fresh laundry soap and aftershave. "I told you I'm not that good," I say with a soft sigh. I feel too content to be embarrassed about my clumsiness.

"You're doing great so far." His whisper fans against my ear, and I shiver. "My toes haven't been stepped on, and you're following pretty well."

I chuckle. "Your standards are very low."

"I'd say your standards are too high. The point of dancing is to relax and enjoy. Nobody's watching or judging."

I tilt my head up and look at his face, following the chiseled lines of the high cheekbones and mouth with my gaze. I want to kiss this man, feel his lips moving against mine. I want to rock my body against the hard

95

cock that's been pressing against me all this time. I want to feel him lose control and come from my touches.

His gorgeous eyes turn darker, until they resemble the deep Pacific, but he doesn't make a move to kiss me.

I don't know what gives me the boldness, but I stretch my body as high as it can go, up on the absolute tips of my toes, and press my mouth against his, my fingers tunneling into his silky, warm hair. I move my lips, softly at first, then insistently, but he doesn't open his mouth. Instead he kisses me back, just with his lips, stroking gently and sweetly, neither of which I want at the moment.

Undeterred, I flick my tongue across his mouth, then almost moan with victory when a low groan vibrates in his chest, stimulating my breasts pressed tightly against him. I clench my fingers in his hair and tug, silently demanding that he give me his tongue.

And he does.

He tastes glorious. Delicious. A hint of tequila mixed with dark chocolate. Our mouths fuse in a drugging kiss, and we breathe each other in. My senses bask in the heady scent, flavor, warmth and everything else about him. White-hot lust pumps through my veins, and I rock against him, my body so wet.

"You do things to me," I whisper against his moist mouth.

"So do you."

"Make me feel good," I say, but it's more of a plea. *Don't let me down.*

"Always." His big, hot hands cup my butt, pulling me upward. I wrap my legs around him so I'm cradling his cock where I'm aching the most. I curse my stupidity in choosing pants for the evening. I should've worn a loose skirt. Then I could've been cradling him against only a thong.

I grip one broad shoulder, my fingers digging into the hard muscles, and use the other hand to tug at his shirt. I want to run my greedy palm all over his naked chest, kiss and lick every inch of his scrumptious body.

It takes more time than I'd like. "Get this shirt off," I demand.

He rocks into my folds. My toes curl, and my sandals slip off, landing with soft thunks on the hardwood floor.

"Your tomorrow's mine too," he says.

"Okay," I answer, willing to say almost anything to get him naked.

He turns so I'm resting against a wall, my body pinned there with his hips. He rips his shirt over his head and throws it on the floor. I immediately reach for his chest, run my hands along the warm, taut skin sprinkled with springy hair. My thumbs and fingers close over his flat nipples, and I laugh when his thick muscles jump.

"You look so scrumptious naked. It's too bad you can't argue in court topless. You could get whatever verdict you wanted if the jury were women."

"That's called an unfair advantage." His nose

brushes against mine, tilting my head up. "Besides, the only woman I want ogling me is you."

Something a bit more tender than I'd like uncoils inside me, and I kiss him so I don't have to think about it too much. I submerge myself in the lust coursing through my body, willing the heat to burn away any sliver of tender or complicated feelings.

I suck on his tongue, nip his lower lip, pinch his nipple. His rough groan inflames me, and I know what I want. "I want you naked," I say, pulling back. "And I want you hard and thick and pumping in my mouth, your back against the wall. I want you hot and mindless. I want to feel you come in my mouth—"

He cradles my face between his hands and kisses me hard. But somehow I can't help but feel he's pulling away, which is crazy. What kind of guy retreats from a blow job?

"You wicked, wicked thing," he says, then gently lets me down.

I hook my fingers in his waistband, but he wraps his hand around my wrists and pulls them up.

"Don't forget your tomorrow's mine," he says.

My alcohol- and lust-addled brain struggles to keep up. "Okay." I reach for him again, but he puts on his shirt instead.

Huh?

I stand there like an idiot, my hands on his shoulders as he slips my shoes onto my feet. His muscles are rock hard, and I know his erection hasn't abated one bit.

He walks me home, which takes no time. The

evening air is cooler, now that the sun's gone down. But it does nothing to cool my heated body. And I can tell his cock's still saluting me, so why is he walking me home instead of getting me naked? Is he having second thoughts about my "no intercourse" rule? But then why should he? He said he didn't mind!

At my door, he kisses me hard enough to almost bruise my mouth. "I'm picking you up at ten." Then he waits until I'm inside before leaving.

I slump against the door, placing a hand over my throbbing lips.

What the hell just happened?

11

I get up an hour early and put on some workout clothes so I can catch Sammi. I know she'll ask me to wait until she's done, but I've waited an entire night. I want Michelle's take on my situation too, but she isn't getting up until at least noon unless a tornado blows the house away. So she'll have to be relegated to being my second opinion.

Thankfully the weather's gorgeous. Sammi would've gone out even if it were pouring, so... I count my blessings, which isn't that hard to do. At the moment, it only takes one hand.

"You want to go jogging?" Sammi says, eyeing my hot pink and white Under Armour shirt and shorts. She's in black Nike leggings and form-fitting top. Even her running shoes are black.

"Yeah. I need to talk to you."

"Must be momentous." She tilts her head. "Can you keep up?"

"Pssshhh. Sure. I yoga four times a week."

She makes a skeptical noise, but starts stretching without discouraging me, and I follow suit. It would be just my luck—Jan's Law—to pull or rupture something while running. Like my Achilles tendon or, if the patterns of the last nine days are holding steady, my hymen. If it really tears, does that mean I'm no longer a virgin? Wow. I could make the Guinness Book of World Records as the only virgin to lose her V-Card during a run.

"So... Did you lose it?" Sammi asks when she's finished stretching.

I choke. "Well. I lost...something." My sanity. Or my sex appeal. I'm not sure which. Maybe both.

"Do tell! Was he good? I bet he was." She starts running down the street, setting the pace.

It's not too fast, and I keep up. "He was good." More than good. Great. Fantastic. Perfect. "But he quit."

Sammi turns around and starts jogging backwards, the better to see my expression. "Uh. He *what?*"

"He quit."

"I don't get it. Did he at least stick it in?"

I feel my face heat, and it has nothing to do with running. "No! I told you I told him no intercourse. But we got all...you know...hot and heavy. And I offered to go down on him, but then he stopped."

She stares at me long and hard. "Did you do something?" she asks finally.

"Like what?"

"Like tell him you're a virgin?"

"Of course not. And even if I did, why would that make him stop?"

Sammi switches back to forward running. "Some guys have performance anxiety. It's a momentous thing to be somebody's first. He doesn't know you've done everything but the cherry popping." She considers. "On the other hand, Matt doesn't look like the insecure type. I bet he can rise to the occasion with extra hard—"

I run closer and elbow her.

"Hey! What was that for?"

"For your pointless speculation!"

"It's not pointless if it's true."

"So, back to the actual event..."

"Oh yeah. Well, that is odd. But maybe you sent out your man-repellent vibe."

"*What?*"

"You do that, you know."

"I do not!"

"You so do. It radiates from you. *NIMP. Don't even think about it.*"

I rack my brain, then give up. "What's NIMP?"

"Not In My Pussy."

I sputter. "No, I don't." We run for half a minute before I say, "Do I?"

"Yes, which is why you still have your hymen."

"Matt's supposed to come at ten to pick me up," I blurt out in my defense.

"Did he say that before or after he pulled back?"

"After."

"Huh."

I wait for her to elaborate, but she doesn't. Instead, she picks up the pace, which is so wrong. I'm entitled to a civilized girl talk with my best friend without huffing and running like a three-legged buffalo. "Aren't you going to say something?"

"I'm thinking."

How can she think and run like a demon at the same time? There's only so much oxygen you can draw in, and most of it's not going to the head because it's needed to fuel other muscles, the kind used for propelling your body forward so you can talk to your friend.

"I bet he's not coming," I gasp, as the distance between us slowly widens.

"Bet he is."

"No." I'm feeling too perverse to agree. And I can't think and run at the same time, not like her. But I know I'm being logical here because why would he come back after that kind of finale?

"Bet you twenty!" Sammi calls back as she makes a turn around the block.

"You're on!" I yell, then collapse on somebody's lawn.

The grass feels like heaven on my back, and I close my eyes, breathing hard. My legs are burning, my lungs are on fire, and my stomach feels like it's on the verge of heaving. I can't believe how pathetic I am. *I yoga four times a week.* Shouldn't that keep me in decent shape?

I'm going to have to lie here until I can move

without wheezing and huffing, then go back home, shower and have a tub of chocolate ice cream for breakfast. Unless Sammi and Michelle ate the last of it, we should have some whipped cream in the fridge too. I can even add some sliced bananas to create a balanced meal. The last time I checked, ice cream contained protein—not much, but enough to make it a meal. I think.

As I slowly recover from the torture, I start to feel just a tad bit sorry for myself. Maybe Sammi's right about my man-repellent vibe. I do get a bit nervous when I'm in a hotel room with a one-night stand candidate. It's hard for me to let go, but does that come across as NIMP? Isn't every virgin entitled to a bit of apprehension? What if the guy's bad at it? Or he doesn't really like you after all? What if he does something really gross or—

Suddenly I stop as hot breaths puff over my hip. I jackknife up, and a terrier barks at me once, his tail wagging. Then he buries his nose in my crotch, making me yelp in surprise. I push the offending snout away, and the dog whines and runs off toward the house whose lawn I've collapsed on.

I prop my elbow on my knee and stare at the dog vanishing inside through the pet door. Et tu, terrier?

Sighing, I get up...and notice that the animal left a wet spot on my crotch. Of course.

It's okay, I tell myself. As far as Jan's Law goes, it wasn't that bad. At least he didn't try to bite me down there or anything crazy like that. He was just trying to investigate if Sammi's right about me radiating NIMP.

I slowly return to the house, which takes me past Matt's place. I eye his BMW. He's probably sleeping like a baby at the moment. After all, it's Sunday. It's unfair I'm the only one up this early... And for what? To get left in the dust by my best friend and intimately assaulted by a pervy canine.

After a shower, I decide I need to go shopping. I should get some sexy lingerie, something powerful enough to negate my NIMP energy field. As I leave the bathroom, I see the sunflower bouquet from Matt in my room and sigh. Today's the kind of day not even sunflowers can cheer me up. I put on an azure-colored dress with a sunflower print—one of my favorites, because I need it—and apply some mascara.

My hair still damp—I'm feeling too lazy and apathetic to dry it all the way—I open the freezer, ready to raid the new carton of ice cream, but it doesn't appeal the way I expected. Not that the chocolate ice cream isn't taunting me to eat it. It is. But it also says if I eat it, I'm admitting that my life is too pathetic to wait until evening for excess sugar and fat.

Damn all inanimate objects that can talk to me tele-pathically.

Annoyed, I filch a granola bar from Michelle's stash and wash it down with some coffee. I feel almost human once the caffeine hits. I go to my room with another cup and fool with my tablet, checking Facebook. An ad pops up on my feed, informing me there's plenty of sexy lingerie you can buy online.

I frown. *How did it know I wanted to buy lingerie? I was just thinking about it.* Ugh. It's *so* unsettling, like Facebook's put an implant in my skull.

Still, maybe the ad has a point. Maybe it's too much hassle to go out. Malls are always crowded, and do I want to deal with people today? Nah.

But I'm not buying from the store advertised on Facebook because that's too creepy. Nope. I'm going to try some other online stores.

After a bit of time browsing, I notice something. Every single lingerie model is young and incredibly well made-up. I lift my head and look at my reflection in the mirror hanging on the door to my walk-in closet. My makeup is sort of plain...only mascara and lipstick. Would I look hot like the models if I put on sexy lingerie? Hmm... I'm having a hard time visualizing it.

Maybe with more effort? I study the models again. Smoky eyes and pouty lips seem to be the way to go. Except I don't know how to do either very well. The last time I tried, I looked like I'd been crying because somebody busted my lips.

Swallowing the last bit of coffee, I go to YouTube to look for tutorial videos. *Wow.* There are like a million of them. Which one's the best? Oh well. I start watching. Apparently smoky eyes and pouty lips aren't the only way to make yourself look hot. I'm supposed to contour too. Then bronze. And... *How many damn brushes am I going to need?*

Suddenly knocks come from downstairs. Sammi calls out, "I got it," so I return to a tutorial on how to apply fake eyelashes so that they look natural. The girl in the video makes it look easy, although I'm not sure how anybody can think the fake lashes she just put on are natural. They are at least half an inch long and would definitely touch the inside of a pair of glasses.

"Yo, Matt's here!" Sammi calls out from downstairs.

What? Why? Oh my God!

I put the tablet down and jump off the bed, almost tripping over the running shoes I left on the floor. Instead of landing on my face, I stub my right big toe against a chair and bite my lower lip so I don't screech like a psycho banshee.

"Ah that hurts, damn it!" I mutter under my breath as I hobble my way to the bathroom to check my face. Just mascara and lipstick. Even if I had the time, I don't have the equipment to pull off smoky eyes and pouty lips. Or contour my face. Apparently that's the key to the fine, sculptured bone structure. Who knew?

My hair's dry enough, so I grab a purse, shove my feet into a pair of comfortable but cute beige wedge heels and twist my hair into a messy topknot before Sammi starts another of her inappropriate inquisitions. For all I know, she could be asking, "On a scale from zero to ten, how do you rate Jan's NIMP?" That is, if I'm lucky and she doesn't think of anything more embarrassing.

Sammi's chortling as I walk down the stairs. *Oh my*

God, am I too late? If so, I'm actually, no bullshit, going to kill her. I swear I will!

I spot Matt. He's looking yummy in a spring-green V-neck shirt and dark slacks. He hasn't shaved, and the day's—or night's—growth of beard looks hot. Hot enough to make my knees weak.

"Sorry I'm late," I say, quickly looping my arm in his. I don't care what I'm late for because I'd say anything to get out of this house ASAP. "Let's go." I tug at Matt hard, but not before Sammi holds out a hand.

"Told ya," she says gleefully. "You owe me."

I frown. "Huh?"

"Twenty bucks." She waggles her eyebrows.

The bet. I dig into my purse and slap a twenty on her palm, then make a zipping motion across my mouth.

She laughs.

"Is there something going on?" Matt asks as he leads me to his car.

"No. It's just Sammi being Sammi."

He opens the passenger side door. "Which is?"

"Inappropriate!" I climb inside the BMW and sit with my knees together. A total lady because well... If I'm not going to be a sexy femme fatale, at least I should be a lady.

Something hot flashes in Matt's gaze, but it's gone so fast I decide I imagined it. My sunflower dress isn't even cut low or short. It's just a...fairly modest and average dress.

He gets behind the wheel and starts the engine.

"Something that requires twenty bucks?" he asks as he pulls away.

I scrunch my face. I don't want to talk about Sammi, but Matt doesn't look like he's going to give up unless I answer. "She and I made a bet."

"Which was?"

"That you wouldn't show."

He cocks an eyebrow. "Why?"

I blow out a breath. Might as well just say it. "Because you kind of stopped in the middle of...you know."

"And I said I'd drop by at ten afterward."

"But...you stopped."

"Yes."

I wait, then suddenly realize he isn't going to elaborate. That's not cool. I hate having to ask, but damn it, I have the right to know if he's just playing games. My face is already hot enough to fry an egg, so why not just go for it? "It's not the same thing. When a guy stops... everything's finished. Over."

He considers. "Do a lot of guys stop, in your experience?"

I choke. "No. They don't." *I* put a stop to it. "I mean...don't guys just want to keep going?"

"Basically, sure. But you didn't want to."

"What?"

"You weren't really into it."

"Are you serious? I was totally into it. I was..." I trail off, not quite able to bring myself to admit how wet I was. Maybe I would've been able to tell him if I were as experienced as Sammi and Michelle. But I'm just me, and I'm too embarrassed to say it out loud.

He runs the tip of his thumb over his lower lip. "I knew you were wet."

Forget frying eggs. You could sear a steak on my face now.

"But I'm not so inexperienced that I can't tell if a woman's really into it or just wants to have her itch scratched."

His gentle yet matter-of-fact tone is irritating, especially because I'm totally, utterly mortified. "Maybe you should've tried to move the needle to 'really into it.'" Ugh, I sound like a total brat, which is annoying me even more. So I add, "Have you considered that?"

"Yes. But pushing you wouldn't have worked."

Is he saying I'm frigid? *Am I? Shit.* I thought being frigid meant you didn't even orgasm. I have no idea how wet and...whatever physical reactions other women get since you know...I've never done it with other women. Is frigidity the reason I've still been unable to pop the cherry? "How do you know?" This time my voice is small, slightly uncertain.

He waits until we stop at an intersection. "Do you know why I'm a good litigator?"

What? When did our topic go from last night to this? But it's probably better than continuing about me being frigid or whatever. "Um. Harvard Law? Summa cum laude?"

He shakes his head. "No. It's because I have great instincts about witnesses. And dealing with a woman is like dealing with a witness...and you were like a witness who didn't really want to be involved."

My mouth turns to an O. Is it good that he's equating me to a witness since they help you win trials? Wait, did he just compare me to a *hostile* witness? I feel my eyebrows pinch. Am I hostile? Maybe Sammi's right about NIMP.

"If you have a witness who doesn't want to be on the stand, you can break her by pushing. It's not that difficult—everyone has a breaking point. However, if you do it too aggressively, you might crack the witness, but you lose the jury's sympathy. They'll remember what you did, how you did it and most importantly, how they felt during and after. And you can bet the witness will too. It's damn hard to win a trial looking like an asshole."

The light changes, and the car moves.

I clear my throat. "You know assholes win more than nice guys, right?" I point out, unable to help myself.

"That's a myth. It merely looks like they win more because they win smaller battles and make a big deal about 'em. But it's the good guys who get the war prize."

I blink. Am I a war prize?

"I want more than one night with you," he says, reaching over to take my hand.

And I squeeze his hand because holy crap, what do you say to that? I'm feeling warm all over, the kind of warmth that makes you feel good to the marrow of your bones.

As we speed along the highway, I suddenly realize I, too, want more than just one night. And the thought is like lightning streaking through me because I've never, ever felt this way about anyone, and it's damn scary.

12

We end up at a dim sum restaurant called Pearl China in Arlington. It's a large airy place and already crowded. The hostess comes over. She's a slim Asian woman in her forties, petite and energetic, and she reminds me a little bit of Aunt Sun. She smiles widely. "Matt! So good to see you."

"Hey, Lin."

"So two people, yes?"

He nods, putting an arm around my shoulder. "Yup."

"Follow me."

Conversations buzz louder as we weave through the restaurant toward a big water tank with flounder and lobsters with rubber bands around their claws. Our booth is a couple of yards away and big enough to accommodate at least four diners.

She gives us laminated menus and leaves. I study it

and check off the items I want on the order sheet. "You seem to know the area pretty well," I say, sliding the sheet across the table to him.

"I grew up here." He marks his choices and hands it to our waitress, who's arriving with a pot of hot oolong tea.

"Really?"

He nods, pouring the tea for us. "My parents practice law in D.C. and Virginia."

Whoa. I did not know that. Sammi never mentioned it...not that I asked, since she seemed more interested in Matt's dating history than his background in general, the kind of stuff that would tell me something about him as a person.

"Then how come you went to New York?" I ask, wanting to know more about him. Everyone in the Darling family does something at Sweet Darlings Inc. Unless he doesn't get along with his parents, it seems logical he'd join their firm.

"Wanted to make something of myself on my own. And at the time, New York felt more exciting than D.C."

Our waitress returns with a cart full of delicious-smelling dim sum plus assorted sauces, then places everything on the table along with a fresh order sheet, just in case we want more food.

When she's gone, I ask, "Is that where you tried cases?" remembering him saying he's good at it.

"Yes. Everyone at the firm had to litigate, although not everyone had a talent for it." He pushes a wooden steamer basket with some dumplings toward me. "Here, try these. They're really good."

"Thanks."

I take a bite and almost moan. It's perfectly prepared, with a delicate balance of veggies and crab meat. Amazing Italian and now this. The man knows his food, and I can appreciate that. I take another, then push it back to him so he can have some before I get too greedy. I'm quite sure that taking more than half would look bad.

"So if you were so good at it, why'd you quit to join Sweet Darlings?" I ask. "I don't know how much cachet we have compared to a big fancy law firm in New York City, and we don't sue much."

Not that I remember, anyway. Alexandra believes in running a tight ship—strict compliance with the law and a corporate culture of adding value. *Profit comes when you add value,* she always says.

"Besides, don't you miss New York?" My cousin Kathleen said she wouldn't trade New York for any city in the world...except possibly Paris or Milan.

"Nope. I don't miss it. I wanted to make a change, and Sweet Darlings Inc. is just the place I was looking for." He finishes his tea, grows a bit thoughtful. "About six months ago, one of the associates at the firm just... collapsed in the middle of a deposition." Matt's mouth tightens for a brief moment. "He never got back up."

The shumai between my chopsticks almost slips and falls on my plate. "Oh my God. I'm so sorry to hear that."

"It was a shame. He was a brilliant lawyer too."

"Is that why you...quit?"

"No. It's just..." Matt frowns. "He had a plan, you know? Pay off his student loans. Marry his college sweetheart. Make partner. But he never got to do any of it, and he was working his life away doing something he didn't particularly enjoy. He might have been a great lawyer, but he didn't especially care for litigation or some of the cases he had to handle."

That sounds so sad. I can't imagine living like that. "Sammi said you had some"—I clear my throat—"less than great clients. I mean, your old firm did."

Matt's lips twist into a wry smile. "That's putting it kindly. It's one reason why I decided to join Sweet Darlings. I like the company, its people and its business. It's something I can feel good about." He hands me a plate of mini-buns filled with minced meat, and I take one. "So if you're wondering when I'm going back to Manhattan, I'm not."

I flush, because he's totally figured me out. Am I such an open book? It's a bit disconcerting because he seems so opaque. Sometimes I think I get him, but there are other times he leaves me totally confused. Like last night when he didn't want me to go down on him. After his explanation, I understand why, but I would've never guessed on my own, and it bugs me that my experience with men is so limited that I'm fumbling around. I start to say something, but a cheery greeting interrupts me.

"Matt!"

I turn my head and see two blondes coming toward our booth. I recognize both of them. One is Olivia, his sister. The other is Emma Beane.

His sister is dressed casually in a Harvard T-shirt, cropped denim pants and red Chucks, looking like a wholesome, American girl next door. Emma, on the other hand, is in a purple wrap dress that shows off her curves and toned legs. Diamonds glitter around her throat and ears, and her Jimmy Choo heels look almost ridiculous on the inexpensive tile flooring of the restaurant. Her blue eyes zero in on Matt, she runs her tongue over her lips as though he's a treat she can't wait to devour...and I decide then and there that I don't like her. Still, I have to admit she's gorgeous, even though she doesn't look anywhere as beautiful as the picture I saw on Google. The fact that she's photogenic makes the situation slightly more palatable, the way a dead cockroach is vaguely more acceptable than a live one.

Matt smiles widely. Maybe he can't really read me after all, even though all of a sudden it doesn't make me feel one bit better. God, I'm so perverse.

"Hi, sis. Emma," he says. "What are you doing here?"

"I was in the neighborhood and asked Olivia to join me for brunch. I haven't had good dim sum in forever," Emma answers, her voice sweet and innocent. So. She's the one who called out his name. "Lin said the wait's kind of long. Do you mind if we join you? My treat."

"I don't mind waiting," Olivia says quickly. "It's only like half an hour."

Thank you, Olivia. Maybe Matt's family is cool, except for the naked dancer uncle.

"Oh come on, we're all friends." Emma laughs like she's said something particularly witty.

Except I'm not your friend. I steal a quick glance at Matt. His face reveals nothing, but the smile hasn't faltered. Not even a little. What does that mean? I need an app to decipher men's expressions. Maybe Sammi and I can develop one together.

"I'm sure Matt's date wants to be left alone," Olivia says.

"Date?" Emma's eyes widen. "I'm so sorry." She finally turns to face me. "I didn't see you there. I had no idea Matt was dating so soon after moving to Virginia. I mean, I guess it makes sense since he needs to marry soon and all, but..." She laughs again.

I give her a thin smile. "I'm sure." My flaming red hair is just so easy to overlook. And what the heck is up with this marriage thing? Is she implying she's going to marry Matt? Ugh. Talk about premature marital fantasy. Surely that falls under TMI.

"You don't mind, do you?" Emma says, fluttering her eyelashes, although I don't know why she's doing that because that has no effect on me. "I mean...unless it's truly a *date* date?"

I shoot another quick glance in Matt's direction. Is this a date? It feels like it, but then we haven't really established any ground rules except for the "no intercourse" thing. We had one dinner and blow-jobus interruptus because he sensed I wasn't ready, so maybe it's just having another meal together and...I don't know. I've never dated a man I was planning to sleep with. Not that I've slept with anyone, either. God. This is a mess. *I'm* a mess.

He looks back at me, and there's a silent patience in his gaze as though he wants me to answer Emma. I can't decide if it's some kind of test, or if I'm over-thinking this. Probably overthinking.

Okay, I'm just going to say no. Olivia alone would've been okay, but not Emma Beane. She reminds me of all those mean, catty girls from high school who thought they should get whatever they wanted just because. This may be Matt's morning, but it's my morning too. And damn it, I'm going to have a great Sunday.

Just as I open my mouth, Emma says, "Regardless, I'm sure she's not one of those insecure girls who can't stand being around accomplished women. It's so unattractive and anti-feminist."

My cheeks heat, and the words I'm about to say get stuck in my throat. If I were a violent person—or Sammi—I might throw one of the steamer baskets in her face.

Matt's eyebrows pinch together. "Emma—"

"Oh, come on, Matt." She touches his shoulder, a seemingly innocent gesture, except I know it isn't. "You know how I get when I don't eat, and I haven't had a bite since I got up." She twists her body this way and that, sticking her tits out and running a finger along his biceps.

Matt pulls back. "That is—"

She reaches for him again, and I want to slap the offending hand hard enough to break her wrist.

Abruptly I stand. I've had enough.

"Jan?" Matt says.

"If Emma's really just *dying* for our scraps, let her have them. I wouldn't want her saying we denied her food or anything."

Emma swivels her head my way. Her cheeks are bright red underneath the layers of foundation and powder. "*Excuse me?*"

I feel her furious blue gaze boring into me. But I'm too far gone to care. "I need to use the ladies' room. The shrimp shumai in particular's really good. I ate almost all of them though, so you might want to have some of the other stuff I didn't bother to finish." I gesture at the table and grab my purse.

As I walk away, my face grows hotter and hotter, my heart beating erratically. I have no idea what just came over me. I'm usually never this catty or mean. And I've certainly never fought over a guy. Ever.

Still, it made me feel good to see Emma's face turn scarlet. I have to hope that Matt isn't too upset—I was too chickenshit to check his expression. Not that it would've meant much, since I can't seem to figure him out anyway.

What wouldn't I give for Michelle's ability to read male-female situations.

I stumble into the bathroom and run cold water over my wrists. Cora swears it helps you calm down when you're upset. Or seasick. I don't know if it works or not, but at the moment I'm willing to try anything to bring my heartbeat back to normal.

The bathroom door swings open, and Olivia walks in. She's impassive as she watches me. Maybe she's mad I treated her friend badly. Given my shitty luck recently, she's probably going to dissolve into cliché and give me that "you aren't good enough for Matt" speech in...*three...two...one...*

She bursts into a giggle, then covers her mouth. "I wish I'd snapped a picture of her expression when you walked away."

"What?"

"Emma! She was so angry, and she deserved it. She knows Matt would never smack her down publicly, so she always acts like a total brat. I'm glad you didn't let her get away with it."

"I see." I eye Olivia warily. "I thought you guys were friends."

She shrugs. "Her father's an important client at the firm, and we grew up together. But she's not the first person I'd think of if I needed someone in my corner." She gives me a small smile, then washes her hands. "Don't let Emma bother you. She's been calling Matt ever since he moved back to Virginia, but you're the one he brought here, not her. I bet if *you* call him, he won't ignore it."

"Why are you telling me this?"

"Because I saw the way he was looking and smiling at you. I think he likes you."

She gazes at me intently, and it's incredibly nerve-racking. I wonder if she's a great litigator too, and if this creepy staring is how she cracks her witnesses. I let out a soft laugh. "I'm not sure if you know your brother as well as you think you do."

"Hmm. We'll have to agree to disagree on that point."

She sounds awfully confident. Maybe it's because she too went to Harvard...unless the T-shirt is a gift from Matt. When did she see all that stuff between him and me? She wasn't watching us that long.

Oh wait. Olivia was at Carlos's. Did she see something there? But that doesn't make sense. Matt barely knew me then.

She sighs. "Matt canceled our brunch, and if I'd known he was going to be here, I wouldn't have come with Emma."

"It's okay."

"No, it's not."

"He and I are just neighbors," I say, because, well... that's what we are. Calling me and Matt something more meaningful seems...presumptuous. Besides, if we were more, wouldn't Matt have told that annoying woman?

"I think he wants to be more. The ball's in your court." Olivia gives me a small nod and leaves.

I dry my hands, reapply my lipstick and draw in a deep breath. Time to face Emma the Nemesis.

13

I run right into Matt—literally, like a sleepwalker into a doorframe—as I walk out of the bathroom. I almost fall, but he catches me, his warm hands wrapping around my arms.

"What are you doing here?" I ask. He definitely did not go to the men's room, because he was just standing there like a rock before I collided with him.

"Waiting for you to come out."

Oh. "You didn't have to do that."

He tilts his head. "Are you upset because of Emma?"

"No," I say quickly. I don't think he heard my conversation with Olivia, but then you never know how thin the walls are, right?

Besides, admitting I wasn't thrilled... Well. That seems sort of absurd. It's like being jealous of who my favorite celeb hottie is dating.

"You're a terrible liar," Matt says.

I cross my arms. "Do you need the ego boost of hearing I was jealous?"

"No. Mainly because you have nothing to be jealous about."

"So if we run into one of my clingy exes, you won't mind?" Even as I ask, I cringe inwardly at how inane I'm being. People can imagine any scenario they want and believe they'd never do X or Y, but until they actually star in said scenario, they'll never know for sure. Not to mention, it only makes sense that a guy as charming and hot as Matt would have an ex. *Plural* exes. I'm the only idiot who's still *intact* at my age, not because I want to maintain my hymen for personal or moral reasons, but because I keep chickening out. A total coward.

My mood plunges, hitting rock bottom. It ought to break out a shovel.

The muscles in Matt's jaw flex. "Actually, I'll be annoyed as hell...and might even consider breaking his fingers if he touches you while you're with me."

I blink at the rough, territorial tone. Even he seems a bit taken aback, from the tight lines that form between his eyebrows.

"But regardless of how we feel, there's nothing we can do to change our history," he adds. "We can only affect our present—and future."

That is so mature. So adult. I've been impossible since Emma popped up. "Okay."

"Wanna get going?"

"What about Emma? And your sister?"

"They know how to feed themselves. No need for us to wipe the drool off their chins or read them the menu."

I giggle. "Do you have a lot of experience with that sort of thing?"

"I babysat once or twice."

"So did I."

He puts a hand at the small of my back. It feels possessive and protective at the same time. Almost unconsciously, I lean into him, absorbing his warmth and scent. If I were a cat, I'd be purring.

Emma spots us and gives me a narrow-eyed look. Recalling what Olivia said—I'm the one he brought here—I want to laugh and stick my tongue out at her, just because. The impulse brings me up short, because it's totally out of character for me to be so...confrontational. But she really seems to bring out my worst.

We stop by the hostess's station and Matt says good-bye to Lin. Then he hands her a few crisp bills. "My sister and her friend are taking care of our bill, but can you give this to our waitress? I was hoping to run into her, but didn't see her."

"No problem. Hope you enjoyed the meal."

"We did. The dim sum was great as usual."

She beams. "Have a great day!"

When we're in his car, I watch him curiously. "If Olivia's paying, why are you tipping the waitress?"

"Because it's actually Emma who's paying. She said she would."

Oh yeah...she did. And I like it that he's not letting

her just say whatever she wants without holding her to it.

"But she's a terrible tipper, even though she works the waitstaff hard."

That doesn't exactly shock me. She probably gets a generous helping of saliva in all her food and drinks whenever she goes back to a restaurant.

"Our server did a great job, so there's no reason to let her get screwed over."

Oh my God. If this were a cartoon, I'd be a puddle with bright red hearts fluttering in the air above me. More than the flowers, dinners and drinks, this is what gets to me—a simple act of kindness and generosity because it's the right thing to do.

"And just to be clear, this *is* a date," Matt adds.

"Oh." I blush. "Why didn't you say something when Emma...you know." I shrug, while squirming.

He sighs. "Because I thought you knew. And I thought you'd set her straight."

"Did you want me to?"

"Yes."

"Oh." I clear my throat. "I was waiting for you to say something." Even though she was really addressing me.

"It's okay to tell people off occasionally."

"And I did."

A small grin tugs at his mouth. "So you did. And I'm proud of you."

My eyebrows hit my hairline. I thought he'd be

annoyed. Don't people hate confrontations? I certainly do.

"And now we're going to continue with our date," he says. "Hopefully, without any more interruptions."

I smile. "Okay."

14

The rest of the day is lovely. We go to Burke Lake Park and ride the train and carousel. I haven't done either in ages, and it's more fun than I remembered. We also get ice cream, because there's probably a law against skipping ice cream on a good afternoon at a park.

Then we rent a boat. Watching Matt maneuver the watercraft with easy expertise is an extraordinary turn-on. I love the way his arm muscles flex, the way the sun highlights his rugged face. The park is public, and we aren't the only people on the water, what with the weather being so nice. But being together in a boat on the placid lake, it *feels* like we're alone in the world.

He leans back and sighs. I sidle closer. "What are you thinking about?" I ask after a moment.

"Socially acceptable version or the truth?"

"How about both?"

He grins. "Socially acceptable version—the weather's nice."

When he doesn't go on, I poke him in the belly and feel the lean muscles contract. "The truth?" I prompt.

"Can I plead the fifth?"

I laugh. "No! You're making me more curious. Come on. Spill!"

A mischievous spark brightens his eyes. "You asked..."

"Yes. Tell me."

"Those clouds over there..." He points. "They look like breasts. Yours in particular."

I burst out laughing. "They do not. You're so lying. Isn't that like perjury?"

"I'm not under oath, and they totally do."

I squint. Well. They look sort of like two circles touching each other. If you have a very creative mind... "They look like Olaf."

"O what?"

"Olaf. The snowman from *Frozen*."

"No, they don't, especially if you look at them from this angle." He tilts his face sideways.

"You're such a perv," I say with a grin. I tip my head back and study other clouds, then quickly cover my mouth when I see a cluster that looks like a...

"What?" he prompts.

"Nothing."

"Oh, come on. You can't have me fess up then not share what you see."

"I'm totally not discussing this with you."

Matt gives me a mock stern look and waggles his fingers. "Are you sure you can bear the tickle torture? Better to say so now."

"I'm sure tickling is against some U.N. convention," I say, pressing my arms against my sides.

"The U.N. isn't here to help you."

Then he's on me. I squeal. The man is an evil tickler, his fingers knowing exactly where to go and how to maximize the effect. I laugh until I can hardly breathe.

"Do you surrender?" he says in a faux Darth Vader voice, pausing briefly.

"Okay, okay! I'm no James Bond. I'll talk."

"A wise decision."

"That over there"—I point straight up—"looks like a penis."

He blinks, then looks at the sky. "Nooooo."

"Yeah, it does."

"It's a rocket, you dirty-minded girl."

"You're totally wrong. Those round fluffy clouds over there are like—" I flush.

He cocks an eyebrow. "See? You can't even defend your position because it's so ridiculous."

"Ha!" I cross my legs primly. "If you hallucinate a rocket..." I shrug, sticking my tongue out.

"You can be such a brat," he says, his tone warm and affectionate.

"What are you gonna do? Spank me?" I taunt. I should be totally shocked that I'm talking like this, but I can't stop myself. He makes me feel safe enough to say all the things I could've sworn I'd never say out loud.

He gives me a wicked grin, gliding a thumb and forefinger along his lower lip. "The idea definitely has merit, but I prefer to start with a kiss."

I look into his brilliant gaze, watch him dip his head. My eyes flutter closed, and I sigh softly against his lips. He doesn't kiss me like he wants to punish me. Instead it's soft, the kind sweet dreams are made of. His scent and taste permeate through me. I place a palm over his warm, scratchy cheek and feel a groan vibrating in his chest. My heart accelerates. My bra feels constricting over my achingly hard nipples.

He slants his head, changing the angle of our kiss. This way, we can delve into each other more deeply. I glide my tongue along his shamelessly, while running my hands over his wide, strong shoulders and chest. My fingers dig into his silken hair.

"You taste so good," I whisper.

"So do you," he murmurs, the tip of his nose brushing against mine.

I pull his head back to me, and our mouths fuse tighter. Sparks of excitement shoot along my skin, and lust thickens my blood until my limbs feel languid and heavy.

My skin grows hot and hypersensitive, and I shift my legs when he plunges his tongue into my mouth with more aggression.

I moan my approval.

Whatever finesse we had earlier dissolves into rough sloppiness as our breathing turns into desperate pants. Decadent bliss pulses through me, and every lick and nip seems to travel all the way down to my swollen clit. I clench my thighs, wanting something—anything to ease the needy pressure building there.

Suddenly a loud honking jerks me out of the hot pleasure. I open my eyes, jackknifing up. The boat rocks, and a pair of curious geese flap their wings in indignation.

I smack a hand across my eyes. "Oh geez."

Sighing, Matt places a kiss on the side of my neck. "You mean, oh geese."

I laugh despite the frustration simmering in my veins. "That's a terrible pun."

"It wasn't that bad, considering."

My gaze slides down, and I see a huge erection pushing against the front of his pants. Maybe I'm shallow, but it's gratifying to know I wasn't the only one lost in our kiss.

I run a finger across his mouth, then stop when my phone chirps twice in my purse. That means it's somebody from work. I glance at it. It's David.

–David: Coming over to Alexandra's for dinner today?

I frown. She hosts a family dinner on Sundays, but we aren't required to go and she's never done it right after a big family party.

–Jan: We just had a birthday party yesterday.

–David: I know, but she wants me and a few others to come. Including you.

–Jan: Why me?

–David: She said she wanted to give you something yesterday, but you didn't stick around.

Yeah, because I wasn't going to hang out with the relatives while going commando.

"Problem?" Matt asks.

"Huh?" I look up, then realize I've been scowling. "Oh. No. Just David asking me if I'm going to Alexandra's for dinner."

I turn to my phone and quickly type up a response.

–Jan: Can't. I have other plans. Give her kisses from me.

I drop it back into my purse. "And I just said no."

"You didn't have to do that."

I give Matt a coy smile. "You don't want to spend more time with me?"

"I do, but if it's important—"

"It's not. She wants me to take some stuff out of her attic."

He frowns slightly. Of course, my simple answer makes no sense because she doesn't need me to move things in her attic. She has plenty of sons and grandsons.

"It's my mom's old things. Letters, journals, photos —you know, stuff not even the Salvation Army will take." I shrug. I would've suggested Alexandra toss them, but she doesn't want to because they're sentimental to her.

"Don't you want them?"

I shake my head. "Not really. I mean, I don't care if

Grandma wants to keep them for herself, but I don't want them taking up space in my home."

A breeze blows over us. Some of my hair has escaped the knot and brushes against my face. Matt pulls it away, tucking it behind my ears, his touch gentle. I look at him. His gaze is clear, without judgment or any kind of morbid curiosity. For some odd reason, I want him to understand why I feel the way I do. I've never experienced the compulsion with anyone before.

"Mom ran away to be with a guy Alexandra disapproved of. She was eighteen. Then she had me. She split with the guy sometime after getting pregnant and before I was old enough to remember anything, because she never married him or had any contact with his family. I don't recall having a daddy or grandparents while growing up either. It wasn't until Mom died in a car accident that her family heard about me. Or so the story goes." I'm not sure if Alexandra honestly had no idea about my existence back then. She seems to know everything else about the family.

"Jan." Matt reaches over and squeezes my hand.

I shrug with an awkward smile, but I don't pull away. "Alexandra thinks I should keep everything and maybe even read through the whole pile, but I'm not sure what I would get out of it. The letters are probably filled with mushy stuff about her crush on my dad, and who wants to read that... Eww."

I scrunch my face to cover up how uncomfortable I am with the idea of learning about the entire circumstances around my parents' running away...and me and everything else. If I look too hard, I'm probably going to learn I'm the reason Mom and Dad broke up. Or maybe I'm the reason why Mom was too ashamed to come back to her family. I don't know for sure, but I think I would've been mortified if I were in that kind of situation, unwed and pregnant with a baby whose father my mother disapproved of. Or maybe it's something worse. It's better that I don't know. What you don't know can't hurt you.

"I wouldn't either," Matt agrees after a moment. "But maybe there's other stuff too, things that might help you understand your parents."

"Nah." I lean into his touch. "She was just a teenager who fell in love and ran off. I think Alexandra wants me to have them as some kind of memento."

Matt doesn't speak. Instead he wraps an arm around me, pulling me closer. I snuggle next to him, absorbing his warmth and strength. They begin to thaw the coldness inside me that thinking about my mom and dad brought on.

And so we stay on the boat and watch the sun set. I wish we could be like this forever. I've never felt so content and cherished, despite the small undercurrent of unsettlement Mom's journals always bring up.

But Mom's in the past. Matt... He's becoming something more.

As the sun turns everything golden around us, I realize why I felt the need to explain—Matt's opinion matters. A lot. And I don't know precisely what to make of that. I've never let myself care much about what guys thought about me—after all, that's what led my mom astray.

Since I turned down Alexandra's dinner invitation, we go to a Mexican restaurant on the way home and have margaritas and spectacular fish-and-beef tacos. The live music's festive, and I grin, watching the musicians with sombreros sing beautifully in Spanish while thrumming away on their guitars.

By the time Matt and I reach our neighborhood, it's almost nine. I expect him to lead me to his place, but instead he walks me over to mine. I tilt my head with a slightly nervous smile. "Just so you know, my house-mates are super nosy." *Ugh*, I think, still keeping the smile on my face in an effort to reduce the damage. That was a total man-repellent thing to say. I should've just asked him to come in.

He grins. "I know. I was subject to Sammi's cross-examination."

I cringe. "She can be...um...blunt."

"I thought it was cute. Obviously she cares about you."

My cheeks warm. I honestly have no idea how to proceed now, what the etiquette is. Both Sammi's and Michelle's cars are in the driveway.

Picking up guys for one-night stands was so much easier. Just flirt a bit, then invite them to a hotel room or something. No expectations or anything like that since I didn't plan to see them ever again. They were just a means to an end so I could pop my cherry and move on.

136

But this is different. Not only am I going to see Matt again, but he's more than a means to an end.

I should just...channel Marilyn Monroe or someone. Just casually open the door and ask Matt if he wants to come in for coffee. Wait. Maybe it's too late for that, and it'd be better if I offered him something else. I have a good bottle of brandy, a graduation gift from Aunt Margo, and she doesn't believe in cheap liquor. We could share that bottle, then kiss and all the rest. Perfect, right?

I reach for the doorknob. As my fingers wrap around it, Matt lays his hand on mine. I stop and look at him, my lips parting softly.

He's so, so close, his body only a hairsbreadth away from me. I inhale sharply and smell the musk and sandalwood from him.

My pulse spikes.

"Tell me to stop now," he murmurs, his eyes searching mine.

I blink. I don't want him to stop if he means he's about to seduce me. I want him to... "Um..."

A corner of his mouth quirks upward, then he kisses me.

In front of my door.

His free hand rests on the spot next to my head, caging me in. I usually feel claustrophobic when a guy does that, but now I feel cocooned, sheltered from the world as we share the space that's our own and sink deeper into the kiss.

He tastes amazing. Even better than earlier. He's

all man and Matt and sweetness and all the things I didn't know I wanted.

I lift a hand and wrap it around his nape, and he strokes deep inside with his tongue. I arch against his body. *God.* He's so insanely warm and hard, and the leisurely way he licks my mouth is killing me little bit by little bit.

Pulses of desire course through me, pooling between my legs. My fingers dig into his neck muscles as I suck on his tongue. The hot liquid need he stoked earlier on the boat swells within me, and I feel like a puddle of melting wax.

"Jan..." He groans deep in his chest. "Tell me what you want."

My brain's slow to process. *You,* I want to say when it finally catches up, but somehow the word gets stuck in my throat. My clit is throbbing, and I'm soaked in my panties, but I need more than his body. I need...

I need... I swallow hard.

He rests his forehead against mine, exhaling a long slow breath. The tendons on his neck and shoulders tighten, then he places a whisper-soft kiss on my forehead, where his was touching just seconds ago.

"Good night, sweetheart."

15

———

Dazed with lust and confusion, I stumble inside my living room. I don't even say, "I'm home." Then I yelp when I notice one of my housemates in the massage chair.

"Good God, what the heck is that?" I say. It's got to be Michelle because her bathrobe is white. Her hair is wrapped in a thick towel and her face is completely covered with some dark green goo, and a slice of cucumber lies on each eye.

"Face mask. It's supposed to make your skin glow," Michelle says, her words slightly garbled since she's trying not to move her mouth much.

"Where's Sammi?"

She gestured in the general direction of the sofa. I see Sammi lying there with the same goo on her face, which is more surreal than Dali's melting clocks. She never, ever does stuff like this. "Why are you covered in that stuff?"

"Seaweed mask," Sammi informs me. "I need to glow."

"Whatever for?"

"To get David to notice me. Then maybe he'll dump that skank."

I shake my head. It's unbelievable that somebody as no-nonsense and practical as Sammi is still pining after my cousin. Objectively speaking, David is handsome, yes, and smart as hell too, but there are other good-looking, smart guys around.

Suddenly, Sammi lifts her head and peers at me. "Why the hell are you here, by the way? Weren't you out with Matt all day long?"

"Yes."

"So..." She gives a sidelong look. "Why aren't you at his place, getting some?"

"He walked me here, kissed me and said, 'good night.'"

An ominous silence reigns in the living room except for the massage chair motor. Finally Michelle says, "Is he, like, gay but in denial?"

"Can't be," Sammi says. "Did you NIMP him again?"

I feel my face heat. "I did not. And NIMP isn't a verb."

"It is now."

"What's NIMP?" Michelle asks as the massage chair completes its program and slowly returns her to a sitting position.

"Nothing," I say at the same time Sammi says, "Not In My Pussy."

Michelle peels the cucumber slices off her eyes. "Wait. You've still got your cherry?"

"Yes," I mutter.

"Oh, that's right. You told him no sex. So why are you upset?"

"Except for intercourse, other things were definitely on the table."

Michelle muses, "Maybe he didn't know."

"I'm certain he knew," Sammi says. "But like I said, it's the NIMP vibe."

"Definitely."

"Why?" I demand, peeved.

"How would you feel if a guy said, 'anything but eating you out'?" The goo on Michelle's forehead quivers a bit. I think she's trying to raise an eyebrow. "This, of course, assumes you like having a guy down there."

My face's gotta be scarlet by now. God, I *so* hate my complexion. But Michelle has a point.

Since I'm not fit company, I drag myself upstairs, shower and put on a long nightshirt with the Sweet Darlings Inc. logo on it. I feel marginally better...but not that much.

Within a few minutes, I hear Michelle and Sammi going to their rooms to sleep. It's almost ten. Michelle needs at least eight hours of sleep, and Sammi will want to get up early tomorrow for another run.

Turning off the lights, I go to bed too, but sleep

eludes me. I toss and turn. Yes, I'm totally horny, but that's not really the point. My B.O.B. isn't enough to satisfy me. I want Matt.

Then why the hell did I choke like that? If I'd just said, "You," at the door, I bet we would've been...doing it. I might've even lost my V-Card by now.

A sudden realization hits me. I do want Matt to be my first. But I want more than just sex. I want more than one time with him, and I need to be certain he's not going to exit from my life afterward. And how am I going to know that unless I ask, right?

Feeling like a stalker, I crack open the curtains on my bedroom windows and check out Matt's house. One of the rooms on the top level is still lit.

Before I lose my courage, I shrug into a light blue wrap, grab a few condoms—the stash I take every time I go out of town—and march over to his house. I pound on the door with more force than necessary, just in case he fell asleep with the light on. It's a distinct possibility. I've done it a few times.

But the door opens quickly, revealing Matt on the other side. He's showered recently too, and his hair's slightly messy. He's in nothing but loose shorts and a shirt, and I step into his house without waiting for him to invite me in.

He closes the door and faces me. "Jan? What's wrong?" he asks.

I swallow. This is it. My palms are so sweaty, I want to wipe them on my shirt, but I stay still and meet his gaze. "Why do you want to sleep with me?"

He blinks, then stares at me like I've lost my mind. I probably have. I didn't get much sleep last night, and my filter's not working properly.

"You're beautiful. And I like you."

Beautiful. That's a cliché, and I know I'm not that beautiful...although he looks at me as though I am. But liking me? That's different. My palms grow even sweatier. My throat is totally parched. I croak, "Why?"

The question hangs between us, and Matt gazes at me with the oddest expression. He's probably shocked. Maybe he's wondering what's wrong with me.

But I have to know that it's not *I like you* as in "I'm saying this because it's probably what you want to hear" or "I'm saying it because it's what's expected of me." I don't want either of those *I like you*s. I've had enough of that.

I lick my lips, my heart thumping wildly. My palms are so damp, I could probably water Matt's lawn on my way back home.

God, I'm being absurd. Why can't I be like most people and just say, "Okay," or even, "Thank you. I like you too"?

Swallowing a sigh, I look away. He's not going to say anything because there's nothing to say. He was probably just being nice because he could tell I'm needy like that. I squirm. The condoms in the small pocket of my throw seem to grow heavy, and my unbound girls and bare bottom feel extra awkward since... Well. I don't sleep with my underwear on. I cross my arms over my chest. I probably should've put some on before coming over. That way it would be less humiliating, even though I'm the only person who knows about my commando status.

"Look at me, Jan."

I take a quick peek through my lashes.

"You say the most unexpected things sometimes."

I clear my throat. "You don't have to say anything. I shouldn't have asked. Sorry." It's really hard to look at the guy when you're feeling stupid and embarrassed. I should've just let Matt set the pace. Surely, he would've said, "I like you," when he was ready, not because I prompted him.

Now he's never going to say it again.

"I don't think you have any idea what I see when I look at you."

He doesn't appear annoyed or mocking. He has the tenderest expression, his eyes soft and dark.

"I like you because you're funny, sweet, unspoiled and vulnerable."

"Vulnerable?" Is that an adorable trait?

"Yes. It makes me want to slay all your dragons and bring you flowers." The irresistible dimple pops on his cheek. My heart knocks harder against my ribs. "Sunflowers in particular."

I stare at him. My brain can hardly process what he's saying. Does he really feel that way about me? *Really?* "Lawyers don't slay things," I blurt out like an idiot because I don't know what else to say.

He shrugs with a smile. "Okay, you got me. I'll *sue*

all your dragons and hit them with so many motions and depositions that they won't know what hit them."

I don't know what that means, and I don't care. Pure, unadulterated pleasure bursts inside me, and since I'm too emotional to come up with clever words, I just fling my arms around him. He's solid and warm, and I inhale soap and his scent. I want this man. I want him to be my first, and I couldn't care less that I don't have my phone to bail me out. I know I won't have any regrets tomorrow morning.

So I tell him. "I want you, too."

"I know."

"And I don't want you to stop just because you think I'm like a, a hostile witness or, you know, take too long to say yes or whatever." I pull back a bit so he can see how serious I am. "I overthink everything and I hesitate a lot. I'm not very good at dating and...stuff."

He runs the back of his fingers along my left cheek, and the gentle touch leaves me trembling all over. "Okay."

"If you're worried that I might want to stop, don't, um, just guess," I add hurriedly. "You can ask me if I want to use a safe word."

His eyes gleam. "I have no clue what kind of experience you've had, but I'm not going to spank you."

I flush. Should I tell him I'm a virgin now? But I want to get this out first, before we switch topics. "I know, but it's really so you don't stop because I'm over-thinking again." My cheeks heat hotter, but I have to say this because he deserves to know. "I wanted you when you were kissing me outside my door earlier."

"I wanted you, too." He tucks my hair behind my ears, his fingers feather-light.

"I, uh, noticed that, but I...I was...um...thinking." And it's that thinking that always makes me anxious... and then Bailey out. It made Matt stop when I didn't want him to.

I don't want to think. Not anymore.

"So what's your safe word?"

"Sunflower. It's my favorite and you're the only person to bring one to me."

And to prove to both of us how serious I am about tonight, I take a step back, shrug out of the wrap and pull the nightshirt off and throw it on the floor.

16

Matt inhales sharply, and I'm feeling totally self-conscious. I've never been completely naked in front of a man before—and the light's pretty bright. Yoga or no, it's not like I have a fashionably lean and slim body like Sammi or Michelle.

Now that I think about it, I probably should've only removed the wrap and let Matt deal with the nightshirt, preferably after dimming the lights. His gaze skims over me, top to bottom then back to my face. For that I'm grateful. I don't know what I would've done if he'd kept his eyes on my breasts or crotch.

"Jesus. Good thing I didn't know you had nothing on underneath," he rasps.

"Oh..." I say, mostly because I'm nervous and need something to do even if it's uttering something as meaningless as "oh."

"I wouldn't have been able to do anything except make animal noises."

And just like that, I giggle, and my nervousness dissipates. God. I don't know how this man always seems to sense exactly what I need. More than ever, I know I've chosen correctly. "Why don't you take off your shirt, Tarzan?"

I want to see him in the light. Our hotel room in New York was kept dim. We also never got to be fully naked since I knew deep inside we wouldn't be going all the way anyway.

But now, I'm going the distance. And I want everything.

He shrugs off his shirt easily. His torso is a thing of beauty—strong, thick muscles, every one delineated in beautiful lines. The wide shoulders and chest taper into tight abs with ridges so defined they could hold pennies. A dark dusting of hair vanishes below the waistband of his shorts.

Licking my lower lip, I raise my eyes to meet his. His blue gaze is so dark, it's almost black. "Are you naked underneath?"

He gives me a wicked grin. "Want to see?"

I nod eagerly.

Holding my gaze, he tugs his shorts down. Watching him take off every piece of clothing for me is incredibly erotic. I don't know why—it's not like he's doing anything to put on a show. But with Matt, every-thing's sexy. Everything feels meaningful.

His shorts hit the floor, and he kicks them toward

his shirt. My mouth waters as I take in the sculpted perfection of his body. His legs are as powerfully built as his torso, his thighs and calves solid with muscles that invite me to run my hands all over. And then there's his cock. I've held it and sucked it, but looking at it with the lights on is different—exciting. It's already hard, the shaft thick and veins pulsing. The plum-shaped head is flawless, and I lick my lips, remembering how hot it was in my mouth, the taste salty and all Matt.

"I love your body," I say before I can stop myself.

The wide grin he gives me makes me flush. "Good. The first time is always a little nerve-racking."

I giggle at his mock sincerity. "Why would any guy with a body like yours get nervous?"

"Because I'm finally with a woman with high standards and a sharp mind of her own."

My cheeks grow hot. It's nice of him to say so, but that's not why it took us this long to get to this point. I couldn't decide, kept dithering and driving both of us insane. It seems like a miracle he likes me after all that.

Matt tilts his head, his gaze probing. "You're thinking."

Am I that obvious? "Uh. A little."

"What are you worried about?"

"Nothing," I say since I don't want to spoil the moment with my inane thoughts. We're both naked, and I already told him we aren't stopping. So it should all be good. Right?

"Come on." He places a finger under my chin and lifts it up. "Tell me."

I bite my lower lip. "It's really dumb."

"Why don't you let me be the judge?"

He's going to find me insane, but I can't *not* tell him either because he's probably patient enough to wait me out. "I was thinking that I couldn't possibly have a sharp mind like you said because I can't even make a simple decision." Suddenly I realize I'm wringing my hands and stop. "I mean, even you knew...which is why you stopped each time."

His gaze softens. He runs his thumbs across my cheeks. "I used to watch Olivia tune her cello when we were growing up."

Wait. He wants to talk about his sister now? Does this mean we aren't going to have sex after all, even though we're both buck naked and he's hard enough to split diamonds? Am I still radiating the NIMP vibe?

"She had to turn each peg, and as she did so, the string would go too high-pitched or too low-pitched until she finally put just enough tension on it. You're like that. A cello that had to be tuned just right before it was ready. There's nothing wrong with being careful or changing your mind."

"Like if I use a safe word."

A corner of his lips quirks upward. "Yeah. Like that."

I sigh softly. This man is so perfect. It's more than his gorgeous face or amazingly proportioned body. It's that his mind seems to be on the same wavelength as mine, always knowing when I need space, and when I need a bit of assurance. "Except there's no need for that tonight. Kiss me, Matt."

17

We move toward each other as though we're drawn by some irresistible force. He cups my face between his warm, dry hands and slants his mouth over mine.

The kiss is languid, our lips exploring each other. Despite the leisurely pace, there is hot intensity seething underneath because we both know exactly where we're headed.

As we indulge in the prelude to what's to come, I flatten my small palms over his pecs, then curl my fingers against the sprinkling of hair. I love the way his taut skin feels and the way he grows more aggressive, as though he can't get enough of me—because I can't get enough of him either. My heart thunders as I run my fingertips lightly across his nipples. A low moan growls in his throat, sending a pulse of lust through me.

He cradles the base of my skull, his hand threading through and fisting into my unbound hair. I gasp, then softly breathe in the warm air between us. I lick his mouth and feel the glide of his tongue against mine. He tastes like minty toothpaste with a hint of fiery liquor. It's headier than any alcohol I've ever had. His skin smells like the best kind of perfume, all Matt with a hint of soap from the shower. It turns me on so much, I don't think I'll ever look at soap the same way again.

His mouth still on mine, he skims his hand along the soft slope of my shoulder, then lets his fingers linger on the sensitive spot at the hollow of my neck. My body goes pliant like warm wax.

He grazes along the delicate line of my jaw. "You're so responsive, so perfect." He presses his lips on the pulse beating at my neck.

My palm rests over his heart, and I feel it thundering *boom boom boom*. My own pulse spikes to match it.

I press forward, pushing my bare breasts against him with a soft sigh. My nipples are pointed and hard, and they throb almost painfully against his chest. Shamelessly, I rub them against him, loving the hot liquid pleasure each drag and pull sends through me.

"Yes. I love the way you use my body to make yourself feel good," he says in a low growl, taking one plump mound in his hand. It feels shockingly hot against my sensitive skin, and I gasp. He kneads it gently, but avoids the hardened, aching tip. I push it into him in an offering.

"Do you want me to play with your nipples, Jan?"

"Yes," I answer breathlessly. "Yes, yes, yes."

He brushes his fingertips along the bountiful swell, then runs his thumb across. Anticipation thickens in my veins, and I can barely breathe, my chest rising and falling fast.

His gaze intent, he pinches the nipple lightly between his forefinger and thumb, then tugs. The slight pain sweetens the bliss coursing through me, pooling in hot, sticky arousal between my thighs.

He leans forward, and my nipple vanishes into his mouth. I let my head fall back, gripping his hair and clasping him tightly to me. His tongue knows exactly how to flick, his cheeks know exactly how much to hollow, and his mouth knows exactly how to drive me crazy with lust. Desperate little noises spill from my throat, and I love the way he adjusts the pressure to maximize my pleasure.

He doesn't let my other breast stay neglected. His hand kneads it, toying with its throbbing tip.

Finally he pulls away from my nipple with a loud pop. It's wet, rosy and pointed. He groans at the sight and flicks his tongue over it again before treating the other breast to the same lavish attention.

I'm lost in the syrupy delight, and he runs the back of his fingers down my soft belly, then follows the path with his tongue and lips and teeth.

"You're delicious all over," he rasps against my navel, his breaths hot on my skin. "All woman and need. I can smell your arousal."

I flush, a little embarrassed.

"Don't be shy. You smell amazing. Musky and

sweet and all that is marvelously you." He presses a kiss right on my pubic bone. "I want the taste of your pussy on my tongue again."

God. It makes me quiver because his tongue is like magic down there, but... "You already did that yesterday." Besides, doesn't he want to do the intercourse? I thought I was pretty clear about what we were doing...

He laughs against my belly. "Jan, we can have everything. I want it all."

"Except anal," I blurt out, my fingers digging into his shoulders. I haven't even done normal vaginal sex, and there's no way I'm okay with anal before the more...traditional stuff first.

His eyes gleam as he looks at me. "Okay." Standing up, he says, "Wrap your legs around me."

And I do. He cradles my ass. The position opens me up, and his cock rests between my slick folds. It's hard, pulsing against me. I tingle all over, and my toes curl. He moves us to the dining table where we had our first dinner date and sets me at the edge. I rest my palms behind me to prop myself up and look at him, my cheeks hot as anticipation sends delicious sparks along my spine. He gazes at me, his eyes dark and intense. I know I'm the sole focus of his attention, and it's so erotic I can barely sit still.

He wraps his big, strong hands around the top of my feet and runs his thumbs along the arches. Holy cow, that feels amazing, and I sigh softly.

"Pink," he muses.

"What?"

"Your toenails." He grins. "I had dirty thoughts involving your feet this morning when I saw you."

I raise an eyebrow. "I'm not sure about toe sucking." Not that I've ever done it, but the idea doesn't get my body temperature shooting up.

He laughs, his eyes bright. "Are you going to say your safe word now?"

"Um. No." I nibble on my lip. "Just stating my preference."

"For your information, that isn't my fetish." He puts a bit more pressure on the arches, and I feel my eyelids go heavier. He seems to know exactly where I need the force. "I was thinking more along the lines of using them to spread you open wide, then tossing 'em over my shoulders while I slide into your wet pussy."

I flush because this thing he's saying? Yeah. I like that. A lot.

"And it's not just your feet I've been fantasizing about."

"What else?" I ask breathlessly.

"Your breasts. They're so pretty, perfectly shaped and sized. When I first saw them, my mind went blank for a moment. The first time it's happened since puberty. Last night, while I was jerking off, I thought about fucking your tits."

My clit throbs. I've never thought hearing a guy talk about jacking off to me would be hot, but when it's Matt talking about having me star in his fantasy? Instant inferno.

"Then imagining my cum all over your chest made me hard again, so I did it again."

"To the same fantasy?"

He shakes his head. "In your mouth. Then between your ass cheeks. Everything dirty and debauched."

"We can do all of it," I say in a pant. I want to do all those dirty and debauched things with him. "Tonight."

"No. All that's for me. This time is for you, to make you feel pampered and well-fucked and thoroughly satisfied."

He wraps his hands around my ankles and spreads me wide. I should be embarrassed, but I'm not, not when I spot clear liquid beading at the tip of his cock. He nibbles along one leg, from the sensitive spot right between my ankle and heel, tracing the curve of my calf to the delicate and slightly ticklish skin behind my knee, and he lavishes the same attention on the other leg. Then it's the same from my knees up, his breath hot and arousing on my thighs.

"Hurry," I whisper.

"I won't be rushed."

"You're killing me."

"The last time we did this, I didn't get a chance to explore every delicious inch of you. I'm going to indulge myself now." He sucks on a soft, sensitive point only a few inches away from where I want him to go.

A long, low moan tears from my throat. The table underneath me is probably getting soaked. I feel vaguely like I should be embarrassed about that, except

I'm too turned on to feel anything but a searing need for Matt.

He places my legs over his shoulders, one hand behind each knee. Impatient, I lift my hips, and he laughs darkly before placing his mouth where I want it the most.

His tongue flicks over my clit, and I shove a fist into my mouth as a white-hot bolt of pleasure streaks through me.

He pulls back. "Let me hear you, Jan. If you must do something with your hands, play with your tits." He waits until I drop my fist, then returns to eating me out. He uses his tongue and lips, knowing exactly where to lick, where to flick and where to lap me up to drive me insane.

The pleasure builds, but he's not giving it quite enough pressure to push me over. He uses his fingers to part my lips as wide as possible, making me hopeful he's going to really push it, but he merely intensifies his teasing.

"Please, please, please," I beg, my breathing erratic.

I'm feeling so achy and empty inside, and the sensation is only growing bigger and more unbearable. Desperate, I use my free hand to cup one breast and tug at the nipple like he told me to. The slight pain hypersensitizes me, but it's not enough to give me the release I want.

Nearly mindless, I say, "I'm playing with my breast, but I need more, Matt. Please."

He rumbles deep against my flesh, the vibration

drawing a keen cry from me. I'm so, so close, and I chase my orgasm shamelessly. He draws my clit into his mouth hard and plunges a thick finger inside. I clench around it. He pulls it out, then thrusts in again, curling it slightly so it bumps against a spot in my pussy that makes my eyes roll back.

"Yes, yes, yes," I chant breathlessly, pinching my nipple hard.

He puts two fingers in, stretching me. It feels so good, and when he scrapes my clit delicately with his teeth, I scream my orgasm, my entire body clenching.

He stands and kisses me hard, smothering my scream. He tastes like me, but underneath that is all him. I dig my fingers into his hair and ravish his mouth. Although the orgasm was spectacular, the emptiness inside me throbs more painfully than ever before and I want this man *now*.

"Love the way you taste when you come," he growls. "One day I'm going to watch you play with your pretty tits and pussy."

"Only if you promise you'll return the favor because I want to see you make yourself feel good and tell me what dirty things you think of."

"Deal." He gives me another hard kiss, then pulls out a condom from his shorts pocket. When I cock an eyebrow, he winks. "I was hopeful when I saw you marching over from the window. I was debating whether to go over to your place or let my palm do the work again tonight."

That's hot. And surprisingly sweet. I kiss him on the tip of his nose, then on his mouth. "Just hurry."

He puts the rubber on himself with swift efficiency before placing his hands on my knees and spreading me. He runs a finger along my folds, slips his thumb into my pussy. "You're so damn tight."

And he's huge. "But it's going to fit." I'm pretty sure it will, because I heard some people even enjoying *fisting*—not me obviously—and as large as Matt is, he isn't bigger than a fist.

He smirks. "Of course it's going to fit. I just need to stretch you a bit and make sure you're ready."

"I'm ready." My body's revving to go, the pleasure from the recent orgasm humming through me.

Laughing wickedly and wrapping a hand around my hair, he tilts my head for a deep, lush kiss, while he uses his fingers to prepare me. His concern is sweet, although he shouldn't have worried since the feeling of being filled is pleasurable. I feel like my body's turning into bliss-goo. I squirm, wanting his cock inside me.

I don't know how long we kiss, but I'm so wet between my legs, I can feel the slick warmth on my thighs. He finally pulls back and licks his fingers clean. "Yum," he says appreciatively.

I pout. "So unfair. I don't have anything to taste." My gaze drops to his condom-clad cock.

He groans. "Later. I promise." He spreads my legs wider, then positions the tip of his dick at the entrance of my pussy.

My breathing shallows, my heartbeat uneven. This

is it. And I'm doing it with a guy I like. A guy who likes me back.

"Watch us," he says, then pushes in an inch and slowly pulls out.

"God," I whimper.

He does it again, each time going deeper. I love his patience, the intense concentration in his gaze as though this moment is the most important one in his life. Watching his shaft disappear into me is super erotic. Although he prepped me with his fingers, having the real thing inside feels completely different. It's more intimate. Hotter. *Way* thicker. My muscles adjust, and I'm so slick, it isn't that difficult for him to enter me. Even the slight burning sensation that starts merely highlights the pleasure of having him inching his way into my pussy.

"Fuck, you're so wet, so hot," he says gutturally, sweat beading on his skin.

"You make me wet." I moan, watching his shaft pull out, feeling the delicious friction against my inner walls. I'm beyond embarrassment. The only thing I care about is making him feel amazing. Even though he said this was for me, I wouldn't have a good time if he didn't. "Fuck me, Matt. I want your dick inside me so bad."

Swearing, he pulls almost all the way out, then plunges in hard, his balls slapping against my skin. I cry out. I expected pain—I'd have to be living in a cave not to know it hurts the first time—but this is kind of stunning.

"Jan," Matt says, his eyes searching mine. "Is this your first time?"

My lips pressed tightly, I nod. "But it's okay. It didn't hurt that much."

"You should've said something."

Something like regret flashes through his gaze, and I stiffen. I have his hard cock buried deep in my pussy, and the last thing I want to see is regret on his face, damn it.

"Why?" I demand.

He dries a single tear on my cheek that I didn't realize was there. "Because your first time should've been on a bed, not a dining room table."

I instantly go back to being gooey because he's being so damn sweet. This has to be the reason I've fallen for him, his ability to be dirty and caring at the same time. "Would doing it on a bed make it feel better? Because I don't think I can get any wetter."

"Jan..."

"I didn't tell you, so you couldn't have known. Unless Virginia has an obscure law banning defloration on dining room tables, it wasn't illegal. You would know that, wouldn't you? You're a lawyer."

He groans, then laughs softly. "You say the damnedest things at times."

I clench around him. "Less talk, more fucking, counselor."

He hisses, but instead of pounding into me like I thought, he kisses me. His hands roam all over my skin, petting me and stroking me, setting every inch they touch on fire. His cock is still inside, hard as steel, but he doesn't do anything with it, using only his lips, tongue, teeth and hands to drive me insane.

And I was wrong earlier. I do get wetter. I'm embarrassingly, utterly soaked.

I pull back from the kiss to whisper, "Please, Matt. You said you'd make me feel well-fucked."

His hands flex over my lower back, and his breathing grows rough. "Damn it, Jan."

"Make me feel well-fucked," I whisper into his ear.

And I know I've broken his control the moment he lets out a rough shout and starts driving into me over and over again. I love the way he feels, the way he owns my body, takes care of me. He doesn't just slide into me, but maneuvers his hand between our bodies so he can flick a finger across my clit, sending fiery jolts of bliss through me with every bump.

I hook my ankles behind him, my fingers digging into his shoulders and my head falling back. An unbearable tension winds up inside me, but I want to hold onto this moment, make it go on and on. Matt cups my breast and rolls the pointed tip between his fingers, then pinches it as he plunges one more time and rubs hard against my clit.

The most intense orgasm of my life erupts, leaving me too breathless to scream even though my mouth is open and my throat is straining. He bucks against me a final time, then comes with a deep groan.

When we've both caught our breath, he carries me up to his bedroom. After setting me on his bed, he gets a washcloth and wipes me clean. I'm feeling too good and languid to be embarrassed. Maybe in a day or two.

"Did I bleed?" I ask idly.

"A little."

I open one eye and look at him. He's scowling at the washcloth. "It'll come out," I say.

"It's not that."

Maybe he's never done it with a virgin before, and he's discomfited by the sight of blood. I want to tell him women bleed a lot more than that once a month, but that's TMI. So I give him an impish smile instead. "We should do it again."

"But not tonight," he says, still frowning. Then he chucks the washcloth into the bathroom.

"I thought there were other things we were supposed to be able to do. Something about dirty, debauched fantasies..."

He mock groans. "You're going to be the death of me. I've created a monster. A sexy and insatiable monster."

I giggle. "Now that I've had a taste of what we can have, I want it all."

He kisses me on the forehead. "So do I." He pulls me closer, pulling a sheet over us, and we cuddle together.

As my mind drifts to sleep, I realize he didn't use any of the condoms I brought. *Hmm.* But it's probably okay. I trust him to provide a good rubber himself. I hold onto him tighter, feeling more content than I ever have.

18

I sense an unfamiliar warmth next to me. My eyebrows pinch for a moment. *Hmm. I don't have any pets...*

The body next to me is entirely too big to be a pet.

The memory of last night suddenly comes back, and I flush. I'm in Matt's bed. I shift slightly and bury my nose in the pillow. It smells like him, but it also smells like me. I smile, secretly happy that our scents are mingling on his pillows and sheets.

As my eyes adjust to the dim light, I take in his bedroom. I didn't pay much attention last night, too sated to care. It's a large room with a sitting area. The ceiling is high, with a fan, and there are two comfy-looking armchairs and a small round table by the windows. Unless my sense of direction is totally messed up, some of his bedroom windows are looking at the man-made lake behind our properties. It'd be lovely to share coffee on a lazy morning overlooking the ducks and geese floating on the tranquil water.

I look around some more. He has three floating shelves with framed photos. I can't see them very well, but they're probably of himself or family and friends. Possibly something artsy. Or not, since he has a huge abstract mosaic art piece on the wall too. It's mostly monochromatic with a few splashes of bright color.

I sigh softly. It's such a manly room. It won't surprise me one bit if Matt has a manly closet too. Wonder if he has cufflinks. Those are sexy...

"Good morning," he says, his voice a warm rasp.

"Morning." I smile, thinking of all the dirty things we can do this morning, then remember today's Monday. "I wish I could call in sick." I gasp the moment the words pop out and clasp a hand over my mouth. I've never, ever played hooky.

Matt laughs. "The thought crossed my mind, too, but if we both call in sick, it'll look suspicious, especially since Michelle's in human resources."

"She and Sammi wouldn't tell." They'd just demand to know all the details. Not that I'd tell them anything. What Matt and I had last night is too special to share with other people, even if they are my best friends.

"Have breakfast with me. I basically only have bagels and cereal, but I can also whip up some eggs if you want."

I don't really eat breakfast, but I don't want to leave

either. So I nod. "Okay. Half a bagel and plain cream cheese for me."

He grins. After placing a kiss on my forehead, he bounces out of the bed, his nude body in full display. I can only see his backside, but when he turns...wait. Is he sporting morning wood? Before I can say anything, he vanishes. Confusion clouds my thoughts. I'm here and naked. Doesn't he want a morning quickie? I'm not against the idea.

Then I shift, sitting up, and wince at the soreness between my legs. It's a bit more than I expected. I'm pretty sure it isn't supposed to hurt this much, since I've heard Michelle and Sammi talk about doing it multiple times. I sigh. Somehow Matt knows and has preemptively showed me consideration again. Maybe he's deflowered girls before, despite his odd reaction about the bit of blood last night.

And because I'm a morbidly curious bitch, I go to the bathroom and see the washcloth flung in one corner. There're a couple of spots on it. So that's my V-Card. Gone.

I thought I'd shout, "Good riddance," when I finally got rid of it, but I feel none of that. Nor do I feel any different. The only thing I'm feeling is relief and gladness that I didn't punch it with any of my previous one-night stands. I can see clearly that none of them would've been worth much. But then I don't know what other man could possibly compete with Matt. He's freaking perfect.

Since I'm not quite feeling blasé about parading in

front of Matt naked yet—last night was a special case—I open a drawer, take out a Harvard T-shirt and put it on. My nipples show a bit, but oh well. Can't be helped. I really wish I had some underwear.

I go downstairs and see two steaming mugs of coffee, a couple lightly toasted bagels and some cream cheese on the table...which has been recently wiped clean, by the looks of it. A small porcelain sugar pot sits in the middle. "Is that from Sammi?" I say, taking a seat.

"Yes." He takes the one opposite me. "And that shirt looks fantastic on you."

I flush. "You like?"

He gives me a caveman growl. "Enough to rip it off you."

I rest an elbow on the table, propping my chin in a hand, and waggle my eyebrows. "You can if you want."

"Don't tempt me. I know you're sore this morning. But next time, you're going to be wearing my T-shirt and nothing else."

I grin, absurdly pleased we're talking about a next time. "Okay." I open the lid on the small pot and dump a spoonful of sugar into my coffee. And it reminds me what I wanted to ask him earlier. "By the way, why did you pick our house? The one on the other would've been a better target." It's owned by a Chinese family, and Mrs. Chang is totally into home decoration and gardening. Their house is one of the most domestic-looking ones on this side of the street, the kind that you know is well-stocked with everything at a single glance.

"Actually... My uncle left me a message, telling me to go to your house. To make sure I complied, he threw out all the sugar and sweetener when I moved in."

I take a sip of the coffee. It tastes amazing. Matt apparently doesn't skimp on java. "What did he say to convince you?"

"He wrote, and I quote, 'They're such young sweet things, just your type.' Except every time he says that, it really means they're hot coeds, just *his* type, and he hasn't exchanged a word with 'em."

I laugh. "That part is true—he never got to talk to us. We did everything to avoid him after his first dance."

"I've told him nude dancing isn't the way to a woman's heart."

"Well. If it had been *you* flailing around naked, it would've been fine." I spread a generous amount of cream cheese on my half of the bagel and start munching.

He looks pleased. "I knew all the working out would pay off."

"I'll bet you're admired by all women in the vicinity when you pump iron." I wince a little at how jealous and possessive I sound. But I can't help it. Matt is *mine*, damn it. If I were King Kong—I can't think of anything cuter, prettier, but at the same time just as fearsome this early in the morning—I'd be roaring and pounding my chest over him every time a woman got near.

Matt sniffs tragically. "Yes. Only as a piece of meat."

I snicker, then polish off my bagel. "Come on. Don't tell me you don't like women ogling your body."

"I want to be ogled for my mind too. I work damn hard on it, even though it's sort of nerdy."

I hide my smile behind my coffee mug. "How nerdy?"

"Very. Glasses, pocket protectors, the whole thing."

I laugh. "You should wear the whole get-up for me one day, make me swoon with lust for your sexy mind."

A dimple pops on his face as he smiles. "If you wear your Clark Kent glasses again..."

"You liked those?"

"Loved them. They looked totally hot on you."

"Deal."

19

Matt lends me one of his dress shirts. It's so big, it looks almost like a real dress on me, the hem ending at mid-thigh. Folded wrap and nightgown draped over a forearm, I walk the short distance between our houses.

I suppose this is the Walk of Shame, although I don't know why it's called that. Shame is the last thing on my mind. I feel awesome about spending the night at Matt's. Like *I want to dance across the distance* awesome, if it weren't for the possibility of slipping and breaking something, which I don't want to do. Plus I'd probably flash the neighborhood en route to a broken bone; I'm still going commando.

Too much thinking again. I'm going to wear the Clark Kent glasses and drive Matt insane with lust so we can spend tonight together, preferably rolling around naked. I suppress a giggle bubbling in my throat because it's such a naughty little plan.

The moment I walk into the house, Sammi calls out, "You got laid!" from the kitchen.

"Yes!" I say.

"Woohoo! Finally! Do tell."

"Well...I lost it. That's all."

"Oh come on!" Sammi says.

"All you have to know is that he was ah-may-zing! And yes, you were totally right about the advantage of doing it with Matt, because him being our neighbor? Perfect."

"So it's going to be a repeat thing?" Michelle says, coming downstairs. She's neatly put together as usual, her brown hair curled into a bountiful bounciness and her makeup perfect. Hmm. I note that although her eyes aren't exactly smoky, she's done something fancy with them to make them stand out, and her face is definitely contoured. New things YouTube tutorials make you notice about your best friend.

I grin. "Yup. Gotta shower and get ready for work."

As I walk upstairs, I hear Sammi say, "Damn. ThaYuMNDo must've been divine. Look at the spring in her step."

"Somebody's got a magic dick," Michelle says.

I giggle, then toss Matt's shirt on my unmade bed and go into the shower. The hot water feels incredible on my sore muscles. But I hurry because I don't have a lot of time. I lingered over breakfast for way too long. If Michelle's ready and downstairs, it means she's there to get coffee and a granola bar. She always arrives at work exactly ten minutes early. Says it's good for the career and worth sacrificing ten minutes of her sacred sleep.

I have precisely fifteen minutes before I have to walk out the door, but that's enough. When my hair's sufficiently dry, I twist it into a topknot and put on some fast and simple makeup since I don't have time to do anything fancy like Michelle even if I knew how. But I remember to grab the pair of Clark Kent glasses and put on a fitted black dress with three-quarter sleeves and a skirt that ends exactly at my knees. I cinch my waist with a thin hot pink patent leather belt and slip into strappy fuck-me stilettos in black.

It's crazy how much I'm looking forward to work. I catch myself humming while driving my Altima to Sweetridge. The traffic's not too terrible, considering this is northern Virginia. Before I get out of the car, I adjust my glasses to a precise degree of superheroic sexiness...then make it to the fourteenth floor with two minutes to spare. Woohoo! Go me!

On my desk is a small box bearing the logo of a local mom-and-pop bakery. I open it and squeal at the sight of a cupcake with chocolate frosting, topped with two pairs of glasses, one blue and one pink. There's no card, but I don't need one to know who left it. I grin like an idiot. This is so adorable.

"That's a pretty cupcake."

I almost flinch when Izzy breathes at my neck. *Ugh.* I do *not* need this. Her breath is like misting hyena saliva. Not that a hyena ever got this close and personal with me, but if we could all shift shapes, she'd be a werehyena with an extra-annoying laugh. I start to wipe the spot at the nape of my neck, but think better of it and use a Kleenex to blot the offending moisture.

"What's the occasion? Your birthday isn't for a couple of weeks yet."

Of course the biggest gossip in the office would remember that. I close the lid. "Nothing." I turn around to face her. She's dressed in a supertight top. I'm surprised her nipples or bra outlines aren't showing. And her skirt... She has to be going commando. Not that I feel the need to personally confirm anything. Ignorance truly is bliss when dealing with her. "What are you doing here?"

"I was just wondering if you heard anything about the opening."

"What opening?"

Izzy rolls her eyes. "You know Dick's secretary quit when he did, which means Matt needs a new legal secretary. Sooo..."

"And you're asking me because...?"

"Because I figure you heard something at Alexandra's party? Duh."

"No. She doesn't talk business with family during social events."

She snorts skeptically. "And your HR housemate?"

"Why don't you ask her yourself?" Michelle hates Izzy, calls her "that worthless loudmouth."

"I already did—this morning—but she wouldn't tell me anything."

Wow. This must be the first time Izzy's come to

work early. She always arrives either exactly on time or slightly late.

"Well…" I give her a saintly shrug and smile. "Sorry. I don't know anything."

"Ugh. So I came in early for nothing," she says. "By the way, why are you wearing glasses these days?"

I shrug. "My eyes get tired after staring at my laptop for hours."

She nods sagely. "Good idea. You gotta be careful about that kind of stuff. No guy likes nerdy four-eyed girls, you know." She sweeps her gaze up and down my body. "Not that you're our new counsel's type. A moment on the lips…" Her eyes slide to the cupcake.

My jaw drops. Good thing she's walking away after that remark, because if she'd stayed a moment longer I don't know what I would've done. Right now, I'm imagining picking her up by one scrawny chicken leg and smashing her face into the concrete floor a few times, the way the Hulk did to Loki in *The Avengers*. Or maybe I could be a wizard like Harry Potter and use a wand to make a piano drop on her. Is there a spell like that in the series? I can't remember. I recall dark magic, but I don't want to be a dark lord—or lady—with a permanent serpentine face (Voldemort really was ugly, even though he was played by Ralph Fiennes) so I'll have to settle for maiming her with the piano.

"Why is there murder in your eyes?"

I start. I was so intent on mentally thrashing Izzy that I didn't notice David walking up to my desk. "It's nothing," I say quickly, pasting on a smile.

He looks skeptical, but doesn't probe. "Alexandra wasn't thrilled you didn't show last night."

"You gave her my regards, right?"

"Yeah, but she really wants you to take your mom's things."

I sigh. "I'll do it. Tell her not to worry." David opens his mouth, and since I really don't want to talk about my mom's things or Alexandra, I say, "We have our bimonthly meeting. I'll get you some coffee and we can go."

He nods. I grab two cups—one for him and one for me—snatch a couple of legal notepads and my laptop from my desk. We go to the huge conference room where the marketing, app dev, and finance teams are gathering. Sweet Darlings Inc. has bimonthly interdepartmental powwows, and they're mandatory so we know what each group's up to. Not all the teams are invited—it's usually on a need-to-know basis to avoid wasting time.

I spot Matt in one of the seats and falter for a moment before catching myself. He gives me a small smile, his blue eyes brighter than a sunny sky, and I feel my cheeks warm. He's so gorgeous sitting there in his navy pinstriped suit, a burgundy tie neatly knotted and lying against a snowy white dress shirt. A pair of supersexy black-rimmed glasses sits on his face, making him look extra yummy. Like, nerd-hot combined with jock-hot. He checks me out just as thoroughly, starting from my face to my shoes then back up. The blue in his eyes sizzles, and I feel his gaze like a silken caress. Delicious goosebumps break out over my skin.

How did he end up in here? I'm pretty sure the legal department isn't involved in today's meeting. It's my job to remember stuff like that.

Still, I can't complain too much. He's seated between two guys from app dev who are happily married, and Sammi's too far away to interrogate him under her breath during the meeting. I take a wheeled chair across from him so I can ogle him from the most optimal angle, with David sitting on my right and a marketing intern to my left.

The meeting's mostly about three new features the app dev team has been wanting to implement. Given the timeline and other constraints, they can only do one before the year's over, and the main discussion is focused on which to deploy first.

I take tons of notes so I can create a detailed executive memo for David. It's one of the things he insists I do.

Suddenly, he says, "Jan, what do you think?"

Uh... I look up from my legal pad. Why is he asking *me?* I'm not an analyst. Still, every gaze in the room swings around, boring into me like so many nails. He's never asked me to speak up in an interdepartmental meeting, and my throat tightens.

"There are no right and wrong answers," he adds. "And since this is a pretty significant feature that's going to take up a lot of our time and resources until the year end, I want to get as many points of view as possible."

Right. Of course, everyone's opinion counts. Except I'm a big believer in keeping my mouth shut and appearing to be an idiot rather than opening it and removing all doubt. But I can't just sit here when everyone—including Matt—is looking at me expectantly. Keeping silent now means I might as well start wearing a scarlet S—for *Stupid*—on my chest.

I clear my throat. "I think the second option is best. It's the easiest to implement based on our architecture, and it'll appeal to our core audience. We can also leverage it to attract a new segment of people who are similar to our main customers. I sent everyone an analysis on that last month, and it's the group I labeled New Target A. I think they can be lucrative, since their taste and socioeconomic status in particular are similar to our, um, core audience."

Doing my best not to fidget, I stop. Cold sweat pops along my spine, and blood roars in my head. I take a sip from a glass of water in front of me, hoping I didn't sound like a total moron, especially in front of Matt. I'm pretty sure saying stupid stuff turns me from sexy librarian into four-eyed idiot.

A quick stolen glance through my lashes shows Matt's smiling. Maybe that's a good sign. *Ugh, David!* Why did he have to call on me like that? I swear, it's some kind of hazing. If I didn't like him as a cousin, I'd probably spit in his coffee tomorrow. I still might, if I end up looking like an imbecile.

"I agree with Jan."

Tim Friedman is the first to speak after I'm done. He's one of the dev app team leads, and he doesn't mince words. As a matter of fact, Michelle told me HR despairs of his inability to sugarcoat his criticism. The only reason developers don't quit is because they think Tim's caustic comments are hilarious. I don't think he's hilarious, but super supportive. And let's not forget sweet. The kind of boss everyone should have. I should use the money I've set aside for David's Christmas gift to get something for Tim instead. He deserves it more.

He adds, "I'm impressed she knew about our architecture, too."

I flush, then clear my throat. "I just read some documents on our Intranet."

Thankfully the leads start talking again, and I'm free to return to note-taking. After a moment of scribbling, I sense somebody watching me, and from the way my skin prickles, I don't even have to lift my gaze to know it's Matt. Surreptitiously I look at him over the rim of my glasses. He's studying me with something that feels like half-lust and half-admiration in his eyes. The temperature in the conference room jumps another ten degrees, and oh wow, maybe I should start fanning my face so I don't end up looking like an over-ripe tomato.

Still, I'm a pro, so I give him a warm, secret smile, then dive back to my task since no matter how distracting and hot Matt is, I still have work to do. I'm just happy I didn't end up looking like a fool in front of everyone.

After the meeting, I gather my things and march out with David as usual. But I really wish we had an excuse to stay behind so I could be in the same room as Matt a little longer. Matt stands to follow, but Cora intercepts him. *Damn it.*

I sigh, but then shake myself mentally. Even if there's no explicit rule against interoffice dating, Alexandra has made it clear she isn't crazy about the idea, so I shouldn't get too obvious with Matt. I don't think it's going to hurt my career here—although rumors would suck—but I don't know about Matt. He's a great lawyer, but Alexandra can be surprisingly ruthless at times. Her motto is nobody is irreplaceable... except family.

Sammi catches up with me, then whispers, "Matt was eating you alive, girl. If you'd just catch his eye!"

"Shut up," I whisper back.

"He's gonna drag you to a nearby hotel, push you against a wall and fuck you silly."

Holy shit. The image is scorching—he's so turned on he can't even take me to the bed. Sore or not, I'd love that because being in that conference room with him, even though there were tons of other people in it? That got my panties damp. But I'm not going to fantasize about it, not when I'm surrounded by a bunch of team members. "Shut *up*," I hiss.

"*Shut up. Shut up*," she sing-songs. "That's so sad. You should come up with something better."

"Okay—shut up and go back to your floor," I say, as I turn left and she turns right. The app dev team uses the entire eleventh floor.

"Yeah, yeah. Lunch. You and me. I'm buying," Sammi says, walking backward toward the elevators.

I raise both of my eyebrows. "Really? You're buying?" Sammi never pays for anybody's meals, and she doesn't expect anybody to pay for hers either, except maybe on birthdays. I'm sure her dates appreciate the attitude, since she can drink like a fish.

"Of course not. But lunch anyway. I'm inviting Michelle, too. You have to come or else."

Sighing, I walk to my desk. Knowing Sammi, she's dying to interrogate me, and my not showing up would be like waving a red flag in front of an overly excited bull. She's developed a spy app that transmits everything, video and sound, to her. She demoed it for me and asked me to install it on David's phone—or his girlfriend's—which I of course declined to do since I'm pretty sure that's illegal. And besides, does she really want visual and audio of when he uses the bathroom and does other gross bodily functions? But I wouldn't put it past her to put that app on my phone in retaliation for denying her a chance to channel her inner CIA.

Just as I reach my desk, David gestures at me to follow him into his office, then asks me to sit down and waits until I do before opening his mouth. "There's something I want to bring up. I wasn't so sure if I should say something, but I'm almost certain it's going to happen after today, and you should know so you can prepare..." He shrugs with a grin.

Oh crap. Is he going to finally propose to the girl he's been dating for the last five years? I mean, I guess that makes sense. Five years is a long time to date if you aren't serious, and he probably wants me to help him locate a good venue for a proposal or something. Maybe even help him pick out a ring, just to make sure it's the kind of rock that a girl would love...although I think he should do that himself because he should know what his girlfriend likes. At the same time, helping the boss is what assistants do, right? And I'm also his cousin, so it's probably in my contract that I'm supposed to help, regardless. Also, Alexandra has repeatedly told me and everyone else that since I don't have any siblings, I'm everyone's honorary sister. Although I'd rather just be a real cousin than somebody's *honorary* anything.

Poor Sammi. She's going to be devastated when she hears. Maybe I should withhold the news until later. If I tell her now, she might do something totally insane. Like bleach her hair white. No, too tame. Breaking into David's fiancée-to-be's house and installing the spy app on her phone would be more like it. Actually, the most probable scenario is going to be far beyond my ability to imagine, because that's just how my bestie rolls.

David's about to talk. I inhale deeply and get ready to act totally thrilled for him.

"It's about the semiannual review," he says.

I clasp my hands, smiling broadly. "I knew it! I'm so

happy for you—" Wait, what? Did he just say *semiannual review*?

He laughs. "I have no idea what you heard, but I'm not up for anything that exciting. I mean *your* semiannual review."

"Mine?" I squeak. I stare at him, certain I've misheard. The person who would review me is David, since he's my direct supervisor, and it's going to be my first at Sweet Darlings Inc. But it's not for another two months at least, unless the dates have changed, so why is he telling me this and why *now*?

"I'm putting you up to be promoted within the marketing team as an analyst. I think you've demonstrated amazing aptitude for it."

"You are? I have?"

He nods. "I know, I know, you said you wouldn't be that good, because you studied finance. But I think you really have a talent for it."

Wow. I had no idea. I mean, sometimes it takes me all evening to do an analysis he wants me to complete. I thought it was David's way of...hazing a new hire. Or some kind of newbie boot camp. Not that I'd ever tell him that, since he's still my boss. "But..." I fumble around for something to say. "We don't have any openings."

"Actually we do." David smiles. "The Marketing VP will have to sign off on it, but I think he will."

Yeah...because that's Uncle Eddie, David's father.

"I know Alexandra asked you to apply for the

opening on the app dev team. If you'd rather do that, I'll support your decision. I want you to be happy."

News travels fast. Did she tell everyone in the company—or just the family? "Great. Thank you, David. I appreciate it. Do you need anything else from me?"

"Nope."

Dismissed, I return to my desk in a daze. It feels surreal. I know it really bothers Alexandra and my uncles that I'm David's assistant. They seem to believe I shouldn't be in such a lowly position. But I don't want to move up the chain just because the family wants me to, instead of because I really deserve to. I'm just not naturally gifted and smart the way they are.

And David pushing me into the analyst position feels like a noose closing around my neck.

20

As noon rolls around, the marketing team members leave one by one to grab something to eat. I put a finger on my lower lip and glance in the direction of the legal department. If I get out of the building with Matt before Sammi calls, I should be okay. Besides, I sort of want him to drag me to a hotel and fuck me silly like Sammi mentioned because that's hot...and because I've been thinking about it constantly after leaving David's office. I even made more typos than normal. *Hmm.* Maybe this is why Alexandra doesn't like coworkers dating. But it's gotta be more mentally healthy than obsessing over a ridiculous promotion I don't want.

Just as I close my laptop, my phone buzzes.

–Sammi: Don't forget lunch! You owe us. I got a table at Jolly Robin.

I squint. Jolly Robin is my favorite burger joint. I'm sure the venue was chosen as a trap to lure me in.

Sammi's MO is no secret, at least not to me or Michelle. Ply me with a good cheeseburger, some fries and a Diet Coke, and who knows what I might spill...

–Jan: Us as in you and Michelle?

–Sammi: Yeah.

–Jan: Can't. I have a lunch date. With Matt.

–Michelle: No you don't. The legal dicks have a working lunch today.

Oh shit. I didn't see that Sammi had looped Michelle into our convo.

–Jan: I thought you guys weren't virgins. What do you need to hear from me?

–Michelle: Post-mortem.

–Jan: Can't do it on a live body...

–Sammi: Shut up and meet us in ten or I'm posting shit about you on the company Intranet. You know I'll do it. I've got some embarrassing dirt on you.

–Jan: You threatening me with HR watching?

–Michelle: I didn't hear anything.

–Jan: I have evidence. I'm screencapping now.

–Sammi: I'll tell them you Photoshopped it. Come on.

I sigh. Sammi isn't going to give in, and neither is Michelle, especially if they went as far as making a reservation at Jolly Robin and checking Matt's schedule.

–Jan: Fine.

–Sammi: I'm driving. Meet in the lobby now.

I make a face. So the interrogation will start before I even get my burger.

Still, it makes sense to take only one car. There's the traffic, and it saves the planet. Sammi has the biggest car—a mini-SUV. Michelle calls shotgun, and I gladly hide behind Sammi. Maybe she won't remember I'm in the car if Michelle distracts her with something. Anything.

But it's Michelle who betrays me once we're seated in the restaurant and getting menus. "So. I heard Matt eye-fucked you during the meeting. I'm sorry I missed it."

Damn it. If Michelle would just keep her mouth shut... "I have to get back early," I say. "David wants to talk about something."

"About what?"

"Interoffice dating rules, most likely," Sammi says.

"We don't have such rules," Michelle says, while studying the menu...which is ridiculous, since we always get the same thing.

Our server comes to take our order. Everyone has their usual—a cheeseburger and fries with Diet Coke for me, a grilled chicken Caesar salad and lemonade for Michelle, and a bacon mushroom burger and spicy fries with pure, unadulterated classic Coke for Sammi.

Our drinks come quickly, and the food arrives soon after, basically at warp speed. But then, nobody goes to a joint where your lunch shows up slower than a slug on tranquilizers, especially on a work day.

"So what's this thing with David?" Sammi asks, licking her lips. I'm not sure if it's over the piping hot food in front of her or the prospect of grilling me.

"He wants to make me a marketing analyst," I say, picking up a fry and munching on it.

"Woohoo!" Sammi lets out a loud hoot, raising both arms straight over her head in a victory pose.

"You go, girl!" Michelle lifts a hand to high-five me.

"But you can't tell anybody," I say even as I half-heartedly slap her palm.

"Of course not. Not until it's official, but what's up with that little tap? You don't want the position?" Michelle asks with a frown.

"Well. App dev *is* much cooler," Sammi says with a wink. "But marketing's not bad. Awesome you're moving up, right?"

"Um. Yes and no. I guess it's nice that he wants to promote me, but..."

"You want to be in app dev," Sammi finishes. To her, only app dev is worth anything, with marketing being second best, and that's only because David's in the latter.

"No."

Michelle peers at me, her fork stabbing a few dressing-drenched lettuce leaves. "Would you rather be Matt's legal secretary?"

I thunk my head on the table. Leave it to Michelle to bring the topic back to Matt. I swear, she's picked up a lot from Sammi over the years. Not to mention, unlike Sammi, who is a bit ham-fisted, Michelle can be subtle. Downright sneaky, in fact.

"No. That would be Izzy Friday."

"That ho." Sammi snorts. "As if."

"But none of this is really the point. I'm just... happy where I am."

Michelle blinks. "Seriously? But you graduated from one of the best undergraduate business schools in the country."

"Yeah. You worked your ass off for it. What gives?"

I take a huge bite of my burger so I don't have to answer them. Talking with food in your mouth is rude. Everyone says so. Michelle and Sammi are civilized interrogators.

Or so I think.

They aren't letting the likes of Emily Post deter them. They wait me out, munching on their lunch.

Finally, I swallow—because I can only chew for so long without looking ridiculous.

"So?" Sammi says. I swear she's been watching my throat.

"I just don't think I'll be good at it," I say finally.

"No fucking way."

"Why the hell not?" Michelle demands.

If I weren't feeling a bit pathetic about it, I'd laugh at their identical expressions—wide eyes, mouths ajar (thankfully they've already swallowed their food), and blinking in sync. "I'm just, you know...not that naturally talented at stuff like this."

"Girl, I know nothing about talent in marketing because that's not my thing, but you're one of the hardest working people I've ever met." Sammi sucks down her Coke to punctuate her point.

"What she said," Michelle agrees. "Look, talent

means nothing if you're lazy. Besides, you aren't a complete idiot or you would've never made it to Comm School or graduated with honors."

I sigh. "Probably not."

"So have some confidence! I don't know why you always sabotage yourself like this. Career is everything."

"Not everything," Sammi corrects Michelle. "Jan has a man."

Michelle shakes her head. "Fine. But relationships come second."

"So. This man-lationship." Sammi gives me a look. "I'm not asking for blow-by-blow because that's TMI... unless you want to share because that's like totally TJI, and I welcome that with open arms."

"What's TJI?" I ask, trying to parse Sammi-talk.

"Too Juicy Information."

"I don't think that's real or grammatically correct," Michelle interjects.

"Nobody cares, except for grammar Nazis, and girl-friend, you just gotta say no to all types of Nazis. Anyway..." Sammi leans forward. "What made you change your mind? Not that I don't approve of Matt—I do, he's perfect—but this whole thing is totally different. It's not out of town, not with a stranger, and certainly not a one-night stand from what I can see."

I clear my throat to hide the smile tugging at my lips. "Well. I like him. And..." I flush, feeling slightly ridiculous and shy at the same time. "He likes me back."

Sammi and Michelle both roll their eyes good-naturedly. "Of course, he likes you, silly. If he didn't, he wouldn't be the man we thought," Sammi said.

"Which is?"

"A smart guy," she says at the same time Michelle says, "A man with impeccable taste."

I have to grin. "Thanks."

"Seriously, I think he should kiss your feet and worship you or something."

I glow. Despite the fact that they can get overly nosy, they're the kind of besties every woman should have, and I'm lucky they're on my team. "I just realized I needed somebody who likes me because he *likes* me, not because, you know..."

Michelle blinks. "What?"

"Because they feel like they should. And Matt has no reason to feel that way about me."

"No one likes somebody out of obligation," Sammi says, picking up a fry and dunking it in ketchup.

"Families do." It slips out before I can catch myself.

Michelle's fork stills in mid-air. "Did something happen over the weekend?"

"No. I was just pointing out an example," I say quickly. I've finished my lunch, including my Diet Coke, so I suck the half-air and half-melted ice at the bottom of the glass hard through the straw.

Michelle's phone buzzes. She glances at it. "A meeting in fifteen. We gotta get going."

Thank you, phone gods.

On our way back, we all sing along to our favorite

Ed Sheeran. I'm not a great singer—dancing isn't the only thing I don't do well—but I don't care. We're all just friends having fun.

As I get out of the car, my phone chirps twice. Shit. My stomach sinks.

"What's wrong?" Sammi says.

"It's Ophelia. She just texted me to come up to the fifteenth floor ASAP."

Sammi and Michelle raise their eyebrows. Ophelia Mason is Alexandra's assistant, and she only contacts you if it's a business matter. And I don't know what my grandmother can possibly want.

"Go," Sammi says. "Good luck."

Michelle nods. "Maybe she's contacting you about the promotion."

My shoulders sag. "Doubtful." Although maybe she is. David could've mentioned it last night while I wasn't there.

We step inside the elevator together. My friends get off on their respective floors. I let the car take me all the way up to fifteen. When the CEO of the company wants to see you ASAP? You go, not even giving yourself the time to drop off your bag.

21

I've been to Alexandra's office twice. Once on Bring Your Daughter to Work Day—even though I'm not her daughter—and the second time when David wanted me to give her some slick marketing plan portfolio that required her sign-off.

But at least those times I was an extra, not a key player. This is different. Alexandra is going to have me do...I don't even know what.

I hope this isn't about the app dev team position she wants me to apply for. Maybe I can deflect her by talking about the possible promotion within the marketing department. But if I do, I'll pretty much have to take one or the other.

Maybe it's Operation Mousetrap. I wouldn't put it past Alexandra. She always gets what she wants.

Ophelia is sitting outside the office, guarding the place like a dragon before a cave full of gold. She's an incredibly put together brunette in her early thirties, her hair the color of dark chocolate that flows down in gentle waves until it reaches her elbows. Her bone structure is amazing. Contoured, I think. God. It's hard to tell, which probably means she's good at it, but she seems to be good at everything. Just look at her outfit—a gold- and turquoise-trimmed coral top, a yellow pencil skirt and teal pumps. The whole ensemble should look actively ugly, but on her, it looks absolutely fantastic.

"Hello, Ophelia," I say brightly.

"Hello, Jan. Did you enjoy your lunch at Jolly Robin?"

My jaw slackens. This is freaky. Does Alexandra's NSA-power extend to Ophelia too?

"Don't look so surprised." She gives me a smile that could be considered warm if you don't mind the robotic practicedness of it. "I saw you go in with your friends when I went there to pick up lunch for Alexandra."

Oh. I guess that makes her slightly less...inhuman. "Do you know what Alexandra wants?"

"Even if I did, I couldn't tell you."

I press my lips together and study her. She smiles at me again. With most people it would be annoying, but not her. She manages to push the smile into creepy territory just enough to negate the annoyance factor.

"Please go in. She's waiting," she says.

Girding my loins, I push the door open and step inside.

Alexandra's office is pretty normal for a CEO's. It's a corner unit with lots of glass and muted pale gray carpeting. The desk is L-shaped and contemporary, and her electronics include a laptop hooked up to a large external monitor and a black gaming keyboard, which one of the app dev team members convinced her to try. The keyboard is currently emitting pulsing waves of purple, pink, red and neon blue.

She's in a pale blue dress with hot pink flowers on her chest and hem. It'd look too tropical beachy on me, but she somehow pulls it off. She gives me that toothless smile, where she just curves her lips up without parting them, and gestures at me to sit down.

"What can I do for you?" I ask. I might as well get this over with rather than let her set the pace of my execution.

"The boxes. I want you to take them now."

My brain falters. What's she talking about? "Excuse me?"

"I'm having them delivered to your desk even as we speak. They're your mother's, and you ought to have them. I'm not storing them anymore."

"But...I thought... I mean... I told you I'd take them later."

"Yes. That was in May." She glances at her calendar meaningfully.

"I've been busy with..." I roll my eyes in the general direction of the company behind me.

"Then I'll have a chat with David, since he's obviously overworking you."

"*No!*" I don't want him thinking I'm saying shit about him behind his back because I'm not. I only *think* he's tormenting me when he dumps tons of work on me, and thinking and saying are two very different things.

"Jan, you've been putting me off long enough. It's time."

"Okay." I clear my throat. "Okay."

"Did you apply for the opening in the app dev team?"

Whaaat? She wants to talk about that now? "No, not yet."

"You should. It's not going to be available forever."

"Okay. But um—"

"If you don't like Tim, that's fine. I know he can be abrasive, but there are other teams available. If you want, you can go to the team located in San Mateo."

My mouth dries. Finally I squeak, "Like, in California?"

She gives me a look. "Yes. It's not the headquarters, but it has some of our best developers, and you'll enjoy the weather, culture and people. I wouldn't be suggesting it if I didn't think it would be a great opportunity for you."

"But...California..." Where I don't have my best friends. Or Matt.

"It's just a suggestion, Jan. You don't have to take it."

"Right." I swallow. "Just a suggestion. Okay, well... Thanks." I stand. "If that's all, I need to get going. We're pretty busy in marketing."

Alexandra's eyebrows pinch for a moment, and she sighs. "All right. Have a productive day."

Is she kidding me? How the hell am I going to have a productive anything after that bombshell? But there's no way I'm saying that out loud, not in her office. Not in private either. "Yeah. You too."

22

Sitting with my legs crossed and a Dell warming my lap, I stare at the papers spread all around me on the bed. It's almost nine, and I'm not even close to being finished with the analysis David wants. The only thing that makes the indignity of working this late slightly palatable is that I don't have time to think about the boxes, which I shoved into a back corner of the garage and covered with an old picnic tablecloth. And the fact that Matt is also stuck in the office because he has some calls with our West Coast people, so I wouldn't have been able to spend the evening with him anyway. And unlike Matt, who's undoubtedly still in his suit, I'm barefoot in my leggings and a super comfy, loose "Keep Calm and Paddle" T-shirt, sans bra.

Well...Matt is probably sans bra, too.

I shake my head and try to concentrate on the fifth bar graph I made for my exhibits. Bar graphs are my least favorite, although a lot of people like them. They look ridiculous, like a bunch of color-coded erections trying to measure up against each other, even though it's totally futile since there can be only one biggest dick on the graph. If you have a tie, you did something wrong—like your data is flawed or your entire hypothesis is wrong in the first place. At least that's my stance, and I'm sticking to it. A pie chart might be better, although I don't think this analysis lends itself to pie charting.

Maybe I should do it anyway. I click around, and the erections turn into pie slices, again every single one of them unequal in size, but they look...sort of not as impactful, and it's hard to compare them on an annual basis. Will David take back his decision to put me up for the promotion if I work a little less hard? Or if my memo is less thorough than usual?

But then that might result in Alexandra shipping me off to Silicon Valley. *Damn it.*

Resting against the headboard, I tap my fingers on my knee. I still haven't told Sammi and Michelle what Alexandra said, mostly because I don't know what to make of it yet. Like...was it a threat—*apply like I told you to or else*—or a promise—*I'm going to ultimately ship you off to California, so prepare yourself?*

To anybody else at Sweet Darlings, it'd look like an incredible opportunity. Who wouldn't want to be transferred to our Silicon Valley office? No one.

Except maybe Sammi, because...David.

And me because...Matt.

I let out a long sigh. Would I feel differently if Matt weren't in the picture? I scrunch my face. No, I still wouldn't want to go. I don't want to be away from my best friends, and in some odd way, the potential move to California seems more like a half-assed cover-up than an advancement. Like how some people shove everything under their bed when they can't be bothered to clean their room.

My phone buzzes. I check the text.

–Matt: Are you still up?

–Jan: Of course, it's not even nine.

–Matt: But I kept you up late. ;)

I flush. Thankfully phones can't transmit that.

–Jan: Work is keeping me up now. You?

–Matt: Most definitely kept up all day long. You were hot as hell in those glasses. And the shoes, and I'm not even much of a shoe man. You also killed it in the meeting. Until you spoke up, the leads were sort of evenly split on the features. They were all good ones anyway. If I hadn't had a working lunch, I would've dragged you away for a nooner.

Damn. I squirm because I would've loved that, too. Anything with Matt would've been great—even if the talk with Alexandra would've ruined my good mood afterward—because he would've been happy. And seeing his dimple is a reward all on its own.

–Jan: So would I, because your glasses were hot as hell too. Alas, I had to settle for a consolation prize. Thank you for the cupcake. It was lovely. And delicious. I started nibbling, then couldn't help myself so I ended up devouring the whole thing.

I gobbled it up after that stressful talk with Alexandra. And it made me feel two hundred times better, because nothing can ruin a good chunk of sugar and fat served with a dollop of sweet thoughtfulness.

–Matt: Want to come over?

–Jan: I'd love to, but I'm working.

–Matt: I thought you were home.

–Jan: Homework from David. Gotta be illegal. At the very least, an HR policy violation.

–Matt: Most definitely. We don't give homework to assistants.

–Jan: Can you sue him for me?

–Matt: Sure...if you come over.

I shift the curtain and see the light on in Matt's house. God, I'd love nothing more than to cuddle with him. Then kiss him. Then straddle him. I don't care who takes advantage of whom so long as I have him inside me.

But...

My gaze lands on the papers around me.

–Jan: Sadly I have to finish the marketing analysis before going to bed.

–Matt: So bring your laptop. I won't do anything to distract you. I promise.

I look out the window again. I can make him out through the open curtains in his kitchen. Matt's standing at the counter, pouring a glass of juice...or something, while glancing in my direction.

Honestly, I don't want to be alone in my bedroom with the papers and laptop. I'd rather be with him, even if he's just watching me work.

My mind made up, I shove everything into my laptop bag and walk over to his house. I make sure to put the glasses back on. No, I don't have my hot sexy librarian outfit on anymore, and my face is wiped clean of makeup, but I don't care.

I knock on his door, and he answers. His tie is loose around his neck, the collar undone and sleeves rolled up. The look sends liquid heat pulsing through me, especially because it shows off the strong column of his throat and the lean muscles flexing in his forearms. I have no idea when I acquired such an appreciation for men's forearms, but Matt's are the best. Not just the best, but the bestest. They should be immortalized in the Guinness Book of World Records. And those glasses? Smokin' hot. Like I have this awesome combination of brain and body and everything else I could possibly want in a man.

I rise on my toes and give him a quick kiss. One of his arms goes around me, the other pushing the door closed. He lingers over my mouth, his lips brushing over mine repeatedly. He tastes like good beer and something sexy and Matt. My fingers thread through the warm silk of his hair, and I lick across his mouth because I really want a better sample. Just one.

Except one turns into two...then three...then four...

My lips part, and I let my tongue glide boldly across his. Lust builds and builds like a storm gathering power. When he flicks his tongue over me and nips my lower lip, I feel it all the way to my clit as though he'd licked between my legs rather than inside my mouth. I squirm, arching into him.

He pulls back, then presses his lips along my jawline. "Good God, Jan, we need to stop if you really have to get some work done."

The reminder dampens my mood, and resentment over the task flares. If the promotion were something *I* wanted, I probably wouldn't be so annoyed, but...

I sigh, collapsing like an accordion that's run out of happy tunes. "I do."

He runs his tongue across my mouth as though to get a last, lingering taste. "Okay. Let's get to work then. I have a few documents to review...and lots of drink options and snacks."

I give him a smile. It really isn't his fault I brought work home, and he's being an awfully good sport.

We share a pitcher of margaritas—strong, of course—and salted nuts. Matt looks super hot, his gaze focused on the legal documents in front of him. I watch him under my lashes, wondering what it would be like to muss him up more and pull his attention away from the papers to me. I'm slightly sore from yesterday, but not so sore that I'm not interested. Beside, if we decide I'm not...one hundred percent recovered, we can do other fun things. Right?

Come on, Jan. Stop fantasizing about Matt and work on your memo. The faster I write it up, the faster I can seduce him.

I wrap up my analysis memo in the next hour, a record for me. But then I've never had such a yummy incentive before. Of course now I have to decide what I'm going to do and how I'm going to do it. It's one thing to plan, but another to execute. It's like dancing. I can imagine how I should dance. I just can't get up and do it without falling flat on my face or bumping into everything.

Besides, Matt's still reading his papers. Unlike mine, they must be riveting. Maybe that's why he became a lawyer—riveting legal documents.

I wonder why I became David's assistant. It sure wasn't riveting coffee runs. But do I want to move up or out to San Mateo? One way or the other, I'm going to be pushed around like a pawn on a chessboard. The question is, am I going to have any say about which square I end up on...?

Suddenly, Matt dumps the documents he's been reviewing and puts an arm around me. "You seem pensive. Problem?"

I cuddle, putting a hand on his chest, right over his heart. It beats strongly under my palm. "Not really. Just thinking about...stuff."

"Anything I can help with?"

His fingers toy with my hair. It feels good, so I rest my head on his shoulder. "How did you know you wanted to be a lawyer? I mean... It wasn't your first choice, right?"

He makes an indecipherable noise. "My first choice?"

Ugh. Maybe I shouldn't have brought it up. What if it's still a sore point? But now that I did, I can't avoid the subject. "The NFL...?"

"Oh, that." He shrugs, the small motion jostling my head. "It would've been nice, but it wasn't my life-long dream or anything."

"But... You could've been a football player. Maybe even won a Super Bowl or two. Don't all guys dream of something like that?"

He chuckles. "Most players don't end up with a championship. Also, it's a very short career. Find me a pro player who's still on the field past forty. So I had something else I wanted to do other than throwing a ball for big bucks."

"Really?"

"I was pre-law anyway, and when I got injured, it was natural for me to focus on becoming the best damn lawyer I could."

"And you are. You were reading those documents like they held the answers to all the problems in the world."

He laughs. "The only reason why I was able to focus is because I knew you had to get some work done. Otherwise I would've never been able to read a word of it."

Warmth unfurls inside me, slowly heating my blood. "Me, either." And because I'm still a bit unsettled about David and Alexandra's suggestion to move me somewhere else—up to and including San Mateo—I cling to Matt. Unlike him, I don't have a backup career.

Trying to ignore the feeling, I tighten my hold around him and nuzzle his neck. "Well...we're done now. No need to hold back."

"None at all." He picks me up.

"We should do some of the debauched things you were talking about last night," I whisper. "Actually, we should do a lot of debauched things."

Matt laughs wickedly. "We'll get to them all, you greedy girl."

He carries me to the bedroom upstairs, his lips on mine. It doesn't take long, his long-legged strides eating up the distance. Soon, my bare feet touch the floor.

I don't let go. My mouth is rough and demanding. I need the anchor and solidness of Matt to help me resettle myself after the day's events with David and Alexandra. Matt bites my lower lip, then comes after me with an aggression that sends liquid arousal pooling between my legs.

We devour each other, mouths fused, tongues tangled and teeth nipping. My hands are clumsy as I work to unbutton his shirt—not much experience with this sort of thing—and I growl in frustration.

I finally give up and order in a low, raspy voice, "Take it off."

His nimble fingers free the rest of the buttons in no time. I push the shirt out of the way; he tosses it over his shoulder. I run my hands over his bare chest, the skin taut and hot. Almost unconsciously, I run my tongue along my upper lip.

"Fair's fair."

He pulls my shirt over my head. My top joins his on the floor in a messy heap. He palms my bare breast, and I let out a lusty moan as white heat streaks through me like lightning. His thumb rubs across one pointed nipple, and I arch into his touch.

"Yes," I hiss.

I dig my hands into his hair and pull him closer for another crazy, blissful kiss. Our glasses get in the way, and I rip mine off and toss them on a table, then do the same with his. Hot need pools between my legs. Glasses on or off, Matt is the same sexy, hot guy I've fallen hopelessly for. It's scary how quickly he's begun to mean so much to me—as though I'm in love with him. Except it can't be love. I mean, how can you fall in love so fast?

But when I drag the backs of my fingers along his thick, hard shaft, and he groans my name, it sure as hell feels like adoration at least. Everything inside me shakes, and I blink away the sudden quake within me because...this is probably a combination of lust and a lot of like between us.

And I can handle lust. I think.

"Take everything off," I say between kisses.

He runs one hand along my spine, the other one still kneading my breast. He slips under the waistband of my yoga pants and cups my butt, squeezing it hard, before pushing the leggings down my thighs. I pull my legs out of them, then unbuckle his belt with a lot less finesse than he's shown. He takes over and gets rid of his shoes and the rest of his clothes.

His thick, hard cock springs forward, the tip already wet. I reach for it, but he takes my wrist gently. "Slow down."

"No." I look him in the eye. "I want to feel you right now. I've waited all day."

"So have I, and I want to make this amazing."

"It already—"

He slips a hand between my legs and fingers me gently, causing my brain to go completely blank. A soft groan rumbles in his chest. "Damn, you're soaked."

"Told you."

But he doesn't lay me onto his bed and drive inside. He runs a finger along my slick flesh, then pushes it in. Deep. I let out a soft moan, and he presses another one into my pussy. I groan, clenching around them. It feels good, but it isn't enough.

"Are you sore?" he asks.

I flush. "Not really."

A small grin tugs at a corner of his mouth. "You're embarrassed about that? After practically begging me to fuck you?"

"It's not the same thing. I can't help it that I'm not embarrassed about wanting you."

"Jesus, Jan..."

Matt's demeanor changes. I watch the way his facial angles seem to grow sharper and harder, his eyes ignite into hot blue flames. It's a huge turn on to witness the effect of my need for him. Whatever I'm feeling now, he's feeling it too.

My world tilts, and Matt deposits me on the bed.

The cool sheet feels amazing against my fevered skin, but not as good as the hot weight of his body over mine. His mouth clamps over one nipple, and I writhe against him, loving the crazy electric sensations his tongue and teeth arouse in me. He grips my ass and continues to work his fingers in and out of me.

"Yes, yes, yes..." I chant softly when his thumb bumps against my clit. Pleasure builds, growing until I feel like I'm about to burst at any second.

His third finger... God, it gives me just enough of the stretch I need. Pleasure bursts, rippling over me like the sweetest honey. Gasping, I clutch him hard.

"You taste amazing." He licks his fingers, then gives me one to sample.

I give it a tentative lick. I've never, ever done that before, and a bit of slick salt coats my tongue. "It's not bad, but I'd much rather taste you, then feel you sliding inside me." I run my forefinger across the tip of his wet cock and put it in my mouth and suck.

He curses under his breath. "You drive me crazy. One minute you're blushing, and the next you're saying things that make me hornier than a teenager."

"That's fair, since you drive me insane too. And you wanna know a secret?"

"What?"

I cup his cheek. "Until you, I've never wanted to say those things to anybody. So do debauched things to me."

Heat erupts behind his gaze. I shiver at the intensity of the fire in his eyes. He kisses me hard, as though I'm a feast for a starved man.

Yes, yes, yes. My whole body screams for him as he rolls me over so I'm lying on my belly.

"On your knees." Anticipation sizzles in my veins, knowing what he's about to do. I shiver as I rise to my hands and knees.

He pushes my shoulders down. "Stretch your arms until you're touching the headboard," he orders, his voice so low and guttural it's almost unrecognizable.

I obey instantly. The position leaves me with my ass sticking up in the air, and my nipples just touching the sheet underneath.

He uses one knee to spread me wider. I hear a foil package rip and bite my lower lip to contain a moan of excitement. I arch my back.

His fingers dip into my opening. "I can't get over how wet you are. How you want me so much."

"Stop teasing."

He runs the slick fingers along my rosette. I tense.

"'No anal' rule still stands," I say just in case he thought it was for only one night.

"I know." He kisses one cheek, then the next. "I'm just getting acquainted with all of you."

He stimulates me there, and it feels incredibly dirty. I wonder if I should stop him, but it feels so damn good that I can't bring myself to put a halt to it. I'm probably a hypocritical no-anal girl, but I can't really be too upset about it. I push against his fingers because I want him inside me.

"Now, Matt," I cry out. "Now."

His hands dig into my pelvis. Then he drives inside me in a single strong stroke. The sensation of having his cock gliding against my pussy walls feels so good, I scream into the mattress.

"No." He stops moving and smacks my ass. It doesn't really hurt, but it stings enough to make me arch my back. "No hiding from me. I want to hear you."

"Okay," I moan my answer.

Only then does he resume thrusting. He's relentless, driving into me over and over again. I always thought being fucked from behind would be a bit impersonal, although probably just as pleasurable as missionary. (Otherwise why would women consent to do it, right?)

But it's not. I can't forget even for a second that it's Matt's cock inside me, and his scent and groans and breathing surround me. He moans my name, calls me beautiful, hot, sexy, his wettest wet dream, tells me all the things I'm doing to him.

Sparks of excitement race along my back, and I cry out lustily. He puts a hand between my shoulder blades, pushing, and my nipples graze against the cotton every time he thrusts. My toes curl at the blissful sensation, and I feel like my whole body's a volcano at the verge of eruption...so close...so close...

His finger presses against my clit, and I scream as a powerful orgasm breaks over me, leaving me wrung out and elated at the same time.

"God... Yes, Jan... Fuck!" Matt drives hard into me one more time and lets go.

I moan. I love the way his cock jerks inside me, knowing I'm the one who's making him feel so incredible. Wrapping his arms around me, he rolls both of us to our sides, back to front. He's still buried inside me, and I treasure the blissful aftermath even as our breathing and heartbeats slowly return to normal.

"Loved it," I murmur.

"So did I," Matt says, pressing a hot, open-mouth kiss on the back of my neck. "Love everything about you."

I still for a moment. Is that what that—my feeling earlier—was? I don't love *him* per se—like I said, it's too early and too fast—but maybe I just love everything *about* him.

And that makes sense. I love his mind. I love his body. I love his considerate nature and everything that makes him who he is. And of course I don't want to lose a guy who I love everything about over some promotion I never asked for in the first place. I lay a hand over his, relaxing in his embrace. "Me, too."

23

The rest of the week passes without incident. David doesn't bring up the ridiculous promotion again, and Alexandra doesn't pressure me about the San Mateo thing. But since I have this feeling that she's expecting something from me—not sure what, exactly—I go ahead and send in my application for the app dev opening with Tim's team. If she tries to move me to San Mateo, I'll tell her I'd much rather work for Tim. No matter how awful some people say he is, he can't be worse than being alone in a new city.

If push comes to shove, I'll resign. There are other companies in the area, and I don't have to work for Sweet Darlings Inc. It does feel strange, though, to even consider another firm. It was always expected that I'd join the company like most of my cousins. Anything else would've been letting Alexandra down.

And after work, I spend my evenings with Matt.

We've done three takeouts so far—since they're quick and easy, and both of us want to spend as much sexy fun time together as possible. But on Friday, Matt texts me.

–Matt: Forgot to mention it, but I got invited to a friend's steakhouse opening. Wanna come? Lots of great food and wine.

–Jan: Love to. What time?

–Matt: Leave around four. It's in Arlington.

–Jan: Got it. Dress code?

–Matt: The way you're dressed is perfect. Love your sunflower pendant.

I grin a little. I'm in one of my favorite dresses—a pale blue number that ends an inch above my knees and comes with a conservative neckline. Since it can be sort of boring otherwise, I'm wearing dangly sun earrings and a big sunflower pendant that rests on my breastbone.

During lunch, Sammi texts Michelle and me. Since I'm leaving a little bit early, I'm eating at my desk.

–Sammi: Happy hour?

–Jan: Sorry. Got a date.

–Sammi: You mean you're going to fuck him. You can do that after a drink or two.

I choke, then shake my head. Leave it to Sammi to get straight to the point.

–Jan: No. We have a REAL DATE. A steakhouse opening.

–Michelle: Oooo, I know the one you mean. Lucky

you. Mom and Dad managed to get a table, but not me. :<

–Jan: Matt said he got an invite.

–Michelle: Can he hook me up too?

–Jan: Doubt it.

As much as I'd love to help her out, I don't really want a date with my nosy friend hovering around.

–Jan: But I'll ask if you can get a reservation there on a weekend soon. How about that?

–Michelle: It's okay. There's no point unless I can get a guy to pay for it.

–Sammi: Pay your own way. That way you don't owe him anything. Unless you don't mind re-banging that guy.

–Jan: Re-banging??

–Michelle: It's nothing. Scratching an itch.

–Sammi: You've been so busy with Matt that you missed it, but Michelle didn't come home until six a.m. last Sunday. Total walk of shame. Or was it a drive of shame?

I can practically hear Sammi's cackle through the text.

–Sammi: I hope he was worth it.

–Michelle: He was good, but not sure about any repeat business yet.

–Jan: Why not?

I have to ask since I'm starting to feel like a bad friend for not noticing.

–Michelle: It's complicated, but I think he likes to lie. And you know how I feel about liars, no matter how pretty they are. Anyway, back to the point. I hate dates who won't at least buy me food and drinks. It's the man's way of signaling he's materially comfortable enough to provide for you.

–Sammi: Geez. Doesn't HR pay its staff?

–Michelle: So? I'm saving my money for bigger things.

I raise both of my eyebrows. She not only works at Sweet Darlings, but also moonlights as a honeypot for a local PI. I thought she was spending all her money on clothes—her wardrobe is worth sacrificing an ovary for —but maybe not.

–Sammi: Like what?

–Michelle: My dream wedding. Mom and Dad are too tight-fisted to splurge the way I want.

–Sammi: Jesus. Hasn't your weekend job cured you of that?

–Michelle: Nope. It's made me more determined than ever to find me the right guy. A man who turns down a young woman who's willing to sleep with him regardless of his marital status... That's hot. I'd totally have his baby.

That's sweet and unexpected. Michelle can be a bit cynical at times, especially about relationships, but I never knew she felt this way deep down.

–Jan: All right. When you find a guy who's going to buy you dinner, let me know and I'll ask Matt if he can hook you up.

–Michelle: Thanks. Enjoy! And take pics!

I grin softly, type "Of course" and hit send.

—Sammi: You're lucky Matt isn't weird about blood. Some guys act like it's the black plague.

That makes me pause.

—Jan: What blood?

—Sammi: Didn't your period start? Mine did this morning, right after my run.

I frown and check the calendar. Sure enough, I'm supposed to start today too. All of us are. After having shared an apartment in college and now a house, our cycles have synced completely to mine since I was the first to go on the pill. After graduation, my period became a bit odd—becoming slightly heavier and lasting four days rather than the usual two—but I figured it was due to the stress of a new job and would return to normal soon. But a total absen—

Sudden panic knots in my belly.

—Michelle: Mine hasn't started yet either. Maybe Jan's body's being considerate, and hers is going to start after she has her fun. *wink* *wink*

The panic subsides. I still have a lot of hours left until tomorrow. And just because our cycles are in sync doesn't mean all of us start at the exact same moment.

The day drags on. I leave my desk fifteen minutes early to freshen my makeup, so I'll look perfect this evening. It's exciting to have an adult sit-down restaurant dinner with Matt. Dim sum was nice, but we were interrupted by an unwanted guest. Let's hope Emma Beane doesn't show up tonight, because she is more annoying and gross than someone changing a poopy diaper on a tray table on a plane. (Yes, I've seen that happen, and it's actually worse than it sounds because witnessing it firsthand also comes with the fragrance.)

"That's kind of a crappy color on you."

I groan inwardly. It's Izzy, making an asinine comment as usual. The coral pink looks great on me—I love the shade, and Matt told me it makes my lips look like luscious tropical fruit he can't wait to devour—so she can suck it and shove her unwanted opinion where the sun doesn't shine. At least I'm not doing cosplay as a hooker.

"What do you want?"

"Did you know Matt's dating?"

I press my lips together and try to look surprised. "Oh?"

"Yeah. It's *so* annoying. I wonder who it is. Probably somebody super good at tricking men."

"Tricking?"

"Why else would he date her and not me?"

I nod. "Right." *Let's just forget how obvious and annoying you are.* "Hey, gotta go. Have a fantastic Friday."

"You too."

When I return to my desk, Matt is waiting for me with a small golden paper bag with a dark chocolate-colored bow tied around it. He looks yummy in a charcoal suit and the burgundy tie I picked out this morning. I try not to grin like an idiot, and totally fail. He waits while I put away my laptop and grab my purse, then hands me the package.

"For you."

"Thanks," I say. "Chocolate?"

He nods. "Belgian, eighty-five percent." He places a warm, possessive hand at the small of my back. I probably shouldn't let him be so obvious since we're at work, but the physical connection feels too good to pull away from.

So I step closer, pressing my side to his. "Wow. That's my favorite."

"I know."

"How?"

He lowers his head so he can whisper directly into my ear. "I asked Michelle."

I shiver as his breath fans over me. My skin tingles where we're touching. I'm almost tempted to ask him if we can skip the restaurant opening so we can go home and continue down the debauchery list before my period starts. But it's the first time we're having a fancy evening date, so I don't want to give that up either.

Given how creative and smart Matt is, we can probably figure out a workaround. If not, we'll have to suffer for four days. Sigh.

"What's wrong?"

"Nothing." I'm sooo not discussing my monthly cycle with him. Besides, he probably knows I'm about to start anyway from the way I'm bloating. At least I think I'm bloating.

As we're about to make the turn for the elevator, Izzy comes out of the break room with a fresh cup of coffee...and stops dead in her tracks. Her mouth is open so wide, if a Dreamliner could fly right into it...which would serve her right after all the catty things she's said.

I shrug, smile, and put an arm around Matt's waist.

He doesn't even seem to notice her. We step inside the waiting elevator.

"You seem to be in a pretty good mood," he remarks.

"Oh, you have no idea. But how could I not be when I'm with you?"

Within an hour, the two of us will be all over Sweet Darlings Inc.'s rumor mill. Maybe I should care—after all, Alexandra doesn't like interoffice dating—but it's damn near impossible when I have Matt by my side, and for the first time since my mom died, I feel content.

24

The restaurant opening is fascinating, and I soak in the whole atmosphere since I've never been to one. Sam's Steaks teems with impeccably groomed, beautifully dressed people. The steakhouse interior is all dark wood, the corkscrew grain adding an elegant and rustic architectural accent. Ceiling fans spin lazily, filling the area with the mouth-watering scent of sizzling steaks.

Matt and I weave through the crowd, enjoying the choice cuts and wines offered to guests during the half-hour reception before the restaurant officially opens. "This is amazing," I say after finishing a bite of perfectly aged and grilled filet mignon.

"Sam knows his steak."

I nod. "I'm dying to get to dinner."

Soon we're seated, and our server brings substantial, leather-bound menus that look like they've been branded. I select the filet mignon, medium rare, with a

Caesar salad. Matt has a rare porterhouse with mashed potatoes. I ask him to decide on the wine, and he murmurs his choice to our server, who nods with a smile of approval. He also orders an appetizer of shrimp cocktails—also my favorite. Did he get the info from Sammi? She knows how much I love them.

Just as our server lays out the platter of huge succulent shrimps, a slim blonde in a royal purple jumpsuit stops at our table. "My goodness, Matt. Finally! I thought about serving you just so we could have some time together."

I look up at her. She's maybe in her late thirties or early forties, her skin smooth and taut over the delicate bones. Something about her feels familiar, and I realize with a start she looks awfully like Olivia.

"Hi, Mom," Matt says with a big smile. "I didn't know you'd show up."

Wait. That's his *mom*?

"I'm here with a client. Zack Beane." She sniffs. "I'm sure *you* wouldn't have shown if you'd known."

"C'mooooon." He gets up and gives her a hug. "Sorry, I've been really busy."

"There's no way that company is keeping you as busy as you say. It must be this young lady." She turns her attention to me. If I remember correctly, both his parents are lawyers. She assesses me coolly, as though I'm a hostile witness. Or possibly some low-life scum she has to defend because everyone is entitled to a lawyer. I resist the urge to raise my shoulders and somehow shorten my neck like a turtle. I haven't done anything wrong.

"This is Jan. Jan, my mom, Melodie Aston."

A diamond on her third finger winks as she extends her hand. "Nice to meet you, dear."

"The pleasure's mine," I say with a smile, pumping her hand a couple of times.

"You'll have to come to brunch tomorrow," she says to Matt, although she's looking at me. "You can bring your date." She shakes her head. "Actually you *should* bring your date."

"Mom, it won't be possible. We have plans."

We do?

"I insist. You've been avoiding me since you moved here."

"Like I said, I was busy, and my answer to your *real* question still would've been a big fat no since I'm not resigning so soon after starting at a new company." Matt is smiling, but there's a subtle undercurrent of displeasure in his tone.

Then it hits me. His mom wants him to quit Sweet Darlings? Whoa. Why?

"Aston Richter Spencer Emerick is your legacy."

"No. That's your baby, not mine." Then he reaches over and holds my hand on the table. "And if you don't mind I'm on a date, and we have plans this weekend."

Except we don't.

Melodie narrows her eyes and glares at Matt, which isn't easy since he's taller. A hostile silence stretches out, and finally I can't stand it anymore. I blurt out, "I honestly don't mind."

"Jan, you don't have to," Matt says at the same time Melodie says, "Thank you, Jan. That's very kind. Matt, it's at ten, like always. You don't have to bring anything."

He gives her a smile just as big as before. "Of course, Mom."

When she leaves for her table, which is on the opposite end of the restaurant, he sighs. "Well. It could've been worse."

"What do you mean?"

"She could've insisted on coming over."

We return to our meal. At least the shrimp cocktail doesn't need to be kept warm. But something's not right. Melodie probably doesn't bite, and she most likely adores her son—I mean, what mom wouldn't if they had a son like Matt? But he seems too reluctant. Maybe I shouldn't have jumped in and forced him into having to bring me to the brunch. Maybe he's worried I'll do something really embarrassing in front of his parents. He knows I've never eaten with the parents of a guy I'm sleeping with. Just what is the protocol anyway?

More or less on autopilot, I take a bite of the shrimp, but I don't taste much of it except to note it's very cold. Perhaps Emily Post has a chapter on dining with your first boyfriend's parents.

"You're thinking too much again," Matt says.

"I'm...I feel like maybe I shouldn't have said

anything. Or maybe you don't want me to meet your parents." I fidget and shift in my seat. "I mean, it's awkward."

"No." He reaches over and holds my hand, his eyes warm. "It's not you. It's really my mom. She thinks I ought to join the firm now that I'm back home, but since I'm not interested, things can get a bit tense. I've been trying to avoid a confrontation with her because, you know, I don't want to hurt her feelings. But I'm not living my life to please her."

"You love her."

He smiles. "Of course. Even when she drives me crazy, she's my mom."

I smile back. That's so sweet, but at the same time, it confirms what I know is true. Everyone does obligatory love, even though they deny it.

And this is why I like being with Matt. He doesn't love me out of obligation. He just loves things about me, exactly like I love things about him.

25

My Saturday doesn't start very well.

Aunt Flo still hasn't come. I'd like to believe she's a few hours late—it's probably still Friday night somewhere in the world—but this isn't like her. If I were a virgin, I wouldn't care so much, but my hymen was pleasurably obliterated days ago. Pregnancy is no longer a biological impossibility.

Damn you, Aunt Flo. I hate you no matter when you arrive!

If she doesn't pop up today, I don't know what I'm going to do. Should I text Michelle and see if she's started yet? It's probably TMI, and she's probably still asleep.

"Hey, you okay?" Matt asks.

"I'm fine."

His hand warms my tense neck. "No, you're not. You've been tossing and turning for the last fifteen minutes."

"Just worried about the brunch," I lie, because I can't blurt out that my period's late. It's only by a day. Not even a full day. Probably a few hours.

Damn it. Starting this month, I'm tracking it down to the nanosecond.

"It's only a meal. Don't sweat it. Just be yourself." He kisses me on the spot between my shoulder blades, then disappears.

A few minutes later, he returns with two steaming cups of coffee. Yum.

"Thank you," I say, wrapping my hands around the mug and its handle. Nothing like fresh java to get my head screwed on tight. Once I'm thinking straight, I'll realize I'm fretting over nothing and jump his bones, rather than letting our Saturday morning go to waste.

Bringing the mug closer, I inhale, then stop as my stomach clenches and my head starts to pound. Stomach response is probably okay. It's probably a signal that Aunt Flo is on her way—which would be great—but the headache? That's odd. Still, I take a sip, then another.

The pounding at my temples doesn't ease. I can only finish half the cup. The injustice! I want to stomp around like Godzilla in Tokyo, except I can't because I have a headache and I don't want to scare Matt off.

Why is the universe against me? Is this another Jan's Law day? I really need caffeine. I need to be at my sharpest.

"You sure you're okay?" Matt asks, peering at me.

"I'm fine. Probably just mildly hung over from last

night." Did I just say that? *Argh*. I wince. Who gets a hangover from two glasses of merlot?

Matt doesn't seem to notice. Instead, he makes sympathetic noises and rubs my temples and back. It helps some, but the headache lingers.

A little after eight, I head home to get ready for the brunch at Matt's parents'. As I shower, I mentally flip through my closet...then realize there's nothing I can wear. A lot of my clothes are too flamboyant or too... something. And I can't pull the look off the way Alexandra and Ophelia can. I'll be like an idiot clown, and I'm sure Emily Post frowns upon being too colorful on your first meeting with your man's parents.

I hurriedly wrap up my shower, then dry my hair as quickly as possible. There's no time to waste.

What do I do? Is it too late to go shopping? Surely something's open. Don't people shop before nine routinely on Saturdays? If not, they should start. Like now.

Michelle's still asleep. I'm tempted to wake her up and borrow some clothes, except she's taller than me, and her girls and hips are more bountiful than mine (she has the perfect hourglass body). I'd look like a fashion-challenged donkey in her clothes. Sammi might be able to help, but she's really into black stuff, which would be, I don't know, too funereal or something. Why am I fretting anyway? I can't wear Sammi's clothes either! She's positively lanky compared to me, and showing up with my boobs crushed into a top a size or two too small won't impress anyone.

But maybe Sammi has some insights. Unlike me, she's done this rodeo before.

"Sammi, SOS!" I call from the staircase.

She looks up from her laptop. "What's your emergency?"

"Brunch with Matt's parents."

She gives me a "you go girl" grin. "Parents, huh?" She props her chin in one hand. "Kinda serious…"

"It's not," I say quickly.

"Guys don't take girls they aren't serious about to meet their folks."

"Theoretically, but this is different. Trust me."

"All right, Miss Luuuurve Expert."

I roll my eyes, and her cheery tone peeves me because her period came yesterday like it was supposed to, while mine's still absent. Bitch. I'm probably the only woman in the world who's irritated she isn't bleeding like a stuck pig on the day she's supposed to meet her boyfriend's parents.

Since I'm annoyed with myself for being less than gracious to my friend, I explain, "He didn't want to go, but he had to because his mom came to our table last night and basically invited him—and then me, when she thought it'd convince him more easily."

"Huh."

"So. Clothes?"

"How formal is the brunch?"

"I don't know. I'm guessing it's just family since it's him and me? She didn't say anything about other guests."

Sammi taps her lower lip. "Okay. Then you need something that's conservative, feminine and can work for both casual and formal."

"How do I pull *that* off?"

She puts her laptop aside, comes up the stairs and goes right into my closet, pulling out a cream maxi-dress with a colorful autumn leaf print on the skirt. "Here. Pair this with a light sweater if it's casual, and a jacket if formal. You can take both and decide when you get there."

I study it critically. She's right. It *can* work, especially if I put on a pair of cute nude wedge heels.

"Thanks, girl." I start putting it on in the closet, while Sammi parks her butt on my bed and keeps talking.

"De nada. I'm sure you're going to impress the hell out of your future in-laws."

I choke. "Shut up." My voice is muffled by the dress.

"Just saying. But I *am* going to be your maid of honor, and you better throw the bouquet my way."

I come out of the closet, pushing my hair out of my face. "You gave Michelle shit about wanting to get married."

"That's different. I already know who I'm going to marry."

Sighing inwardly, I start putting on my makeup. "What are you going to do if David marries his current girlfriend?"

Sammi hisses. "Blasphemy!"

"They've been together for five years. That's a long time."

"Fine. In that case, I'll become a nun."

"You know they eat nothing but white bread and water?"

She waves a hand. "As long as there's Wi-Fi."

I shake my head. Her obsession with David just kills me because it's so weird. If I were hung up on a guy, I don't think I could date anyone else, but she does. As she put it, she's not shelving her life for a man. So what's up with her desire now to marry him and no one else?

I put on the shoes and decide to wait for Matt on the massage chair. Sammi and I share the chocolate I got from Matt. It's so rich, it melts in my mouth like buttery clouds.

"Damn, this is good," Sammi says.

"Yup."

"You really lucked out."

"Yup."

No matter what happens, I can't ever regret what I have with Matt. A smart man who makes you laugh and orgasm multiple times a night?

He's a keeper.

I flinch at the sudden thought. Well. He's a keeper if he wants to be kept, but we only said we liked things about each other. And it's too soon. And we're neighbors and coworkers, and it's always best to go slow. Isn't life a marathon? I bet romantic relationships are too.

Just as the massage chair's full-body cycle has

finished, Matt shows up. He's dressed semi-casually in a V-neck shirt, sleeves rolled up to his elbows to show off his delicious forearms, and slacks. I feel immensely relieved about my outfit.

"How's the headache?" he asks me after a soft kiss on my forehead.

"Much better."

"Glad to hear that, but if you aren't feeling well, you don't have to go."

Despite the concern in his gaze, his lips are set in a tight line. Sudden awkwardness makes me shut up. Contrary to what he said, he's probably unhappy I accepted the invitation—sort of. I mean, eating with his parents means we aren't doing a marathon. Even if it isn't fast enough to be a sprint, it's at least a middle-distance event.

"Maybe after the brunch, we can do something fun together," I say with a lascivious look, waggling my eyebrows.

He laughs, then leers back at me. "Deal."

Matt's parents' house is in McLean. It's a stately stone and brick building. The roof has a couple of pointy peaks. Like other homes in the subdivision, this one has two chimneys, probably to make extra sure Santa doesn't miss it on Christmas Eve. I can see kids in the neighborhood getting double the presents of everyone else. McLean has some of the most expensive and luxurious homes in the entire country. It caters to diplomats, members of Congress and other high-ranking government officials.

Matt leads me to the house. The foyer is grand, with lots of smooth stones, a soaring ceiling with a chandelier and arched doorways. The entire place is spotless, as though it's being shown on the market.

Melodie comes out of the kitchen to greet us. She's dressed in a chic pearl gray dress that brings out her eyes, and her sleek hair is unbound, shimmering like gold over her shoulders. She hugs Matt, kissing him on both cheeks. Then she hugs me and gives me air kisses. Even though it isn't that strong, the cloud of perfume on her brings my headache back. Still, I force a friendly smile.

"So glad you could finally make it." She turns to the kitchen. "Honey, Matt's home!"

"Coming." A tall, broad-shouldered man comes out with a mug of coffee. Dark hair. Big muscular body. Deep blue eyes. Yup. Matt wasn't kidding when he said he took after his father. The man's in a navy polo shirt and dark brown pants. He and Matt do the man-hug, each putting an arm around the other and slapping the other's back once or twice.

I look at both, then my eyes almost bug out when I spot the black letters on Matt's dad's white mug:

A

R

S

E

I choke.

"What's wrong, dear?" Melodie asks.

There's no way I can tell her. It could be that Matt's dad doesn't know what "arse" means.

No, he's a lawyer. Of course he knows. He probably knows how to say that in Latin too. Our previous legal dick—the one Matt replaced—certainly did.

"Let's get her something to drink," Matt's dad says. "I'm Steve, Jan. I've heard a lot about you from my wife."

He has? What does Melodie know about *me*? "Nice to meet you," I say, since I can't think of anything else.

He shifts, and I see the rest of the mug. It's not ARSE written on the outside. It's actually Aston Richter Spencer Emerick, one name per line, which is why I only saw the ARSE at first.

Steve grins. "Cool mug, huh? The firm."

"It's a *great* mug," I say. "Perfect size for coffee."

"Exactly! That's what I said when I chose this style."

"We really need to have Spencer and Emerick switch their names," Melodie says with a small frown.

Steve snorts. "Good luck with Spencer's ego in the way." He gestures. "Come on. Let's eat. We have pancakes, bacon and eggs, plus tons of pastries."

My mouth waters. Pancakes sound fantastic.

Except when we actually get to the dining room, and I see the food spread out, my appetite dies a painful death. Everything looks pretty...unappetizing.

It's not because the presentation is horrible. The food is laid out with a generous amount of fresh berries, powdered sugar, whipped cream and maple syrup. It can't get much prettier than this.

Maybe it's the décor. The room looks like a miniature St. Peter's Basilica with intricate murals on the paneled ceiling, although Michelangelo probably had nothing to do with it.

I'm probably just not used to this kind of...grandness in most people's homes. Everyone else seems fine. "Serve yourself," Melodie says. "We have plenty, so take as much as you want."

I take a plate and hesitate. Why couldn't she have made just enough for us and then served a set portion? *But no...*

How much am I supposed to take? Not taking any would be an insult, but I don't want to waste food either. Is she going to think I'm a picky eater or...worse? God, I wish I had an app that can tell me so I don't end up making an ass out of myself in front of Matt's parents.

"Everything's going to be good," Matt whispers into my ear. "Mom's an excellent cook."

Right. He had to get his cooking skill from somebody.

The weight of the Astons' gazes pressing upon me, I help myself to one of everything plus a small spoonful of scrambled eggs, then take a seat next to Matt, who has brought a mountain of food to match his manppetite.

"Coffee?" Melodie asks.

I should have some, but the idea makes my stomach turn in an ugly way. What's wrong with me? "I'll have some orange juice, if you don't mind."

Steve brings out a pitcher and serves me. I sip my OJ, which goes down smoothly, then start moving food around on the plate, hoping nobody notices I'm not actually eating.

"Is anything not to your liking?" Melodie asks me after a few moments.

"Um. No. It's all good."

"You haven't had a single bite."

Oh my God. Has she been watching me that closely?

Gad. This is probably how she taught the little Matt all the ways to break a witness. The skill is something you have to learn as a child, I suspect because I can't do it.

"She hasn't been feeling well since this morning," Matt says.

"Ah." Melodie raises both of her eyebrows. "Problems at work?"

If you want to consider possible promotions and a relocation I don't want problems... "Something like that."

"What do you do?" she asks, leaning slightly forward.

Geez. I thought she told a lot about me to her husband. On the other hand, not everyone has a friend like Sammi who'll do all the digging for you. "I'm an assistant to a marketing manager at Sweet Darlings Inc."

"Oh." She frowns, then gives Matt a subtle look. I can't quite decipher it, but it isn't full of approval. More like surprise and something else unflattering. "An *assistant*."

"It's a great job. I love my boss." Except when he gives me lots of homework or puts me up for a promotion I don't want. But Melodie doesn't need to know that part. Nobody does.

"I'm sure. Which marketing person do you work for?"

"David Darling."

"Not a terrible choice. I hear nice things about him. An ambitious young man. He went to Harvard, too, just like Matt. We keep up with the alumni news."

If this is a subtle dig that I didn't go to Harvard like David, she missed the mark. I've already accepted that I'm never going to be as cool as my cousins. "He's a good guy."

"How did you meet my son?"

"Mother," Matt says.

I give him a small smile. "It's okay." Her questions are nowhere as intrusive as Sammi's would've been. Besides, I'm sure his mom didn't invite me to just feed me. Don't parents want to know what's going on with their kids? She probably wants to make sure I'm not a bad influence, the kind of girlfriend who'll lead her son to do drugs, get wild tattoos—or get dogs, joint custody.

"In New York," I say at the same time Matt says, "At work."

Her eyes sharpen. Uh-oh. Is this where she starts cross-examining me? "Which is it?" she asks sweetly.

"We met in New York briefly right before I was leaving, and then we ran into each other at Sweet Darlings Inc.," Matt clarifies. "It's like fate."

Steve merely grunts, while Melodie laughs. "You can be so funny for a lawyer."

"I'm not being funny."

"Oh, shush." She waves at him, then turns her attention back to me. "Surely, you don't plan to be an assistant forever? Maybe move up to another, more meaningful track?"

My jaw drops. Et tu, Melodie? Why are people so interested in my career?

Did Alexandra hire her to talk to me about doing something else? My grandmother has undoubtedly heard about me and Matt. Izzy isn't the type to keep gossip to herself. And if she couldn't have him for herself, being the first person to know who he's dating would be a pretty good consolation prize.

"She will, when it's time," Matt interjects. "After all, she's Alexandra Darling's youngest grandchild."

One of Melodie's expensively shaped eyebrows arches. "Reeeeally?" When she opens her mouth, the doorbell rings. She frowns, but gets up anyway to see who it is.

I sip my juice and inhale deeply. Maybe Melodie won't be asking any more questions. This breakfast was a terrible idea. What was I thinking? The headache, lack of appetite and the anxiety over Aunt No-Show Flo aren't helping.

But I should've known better than to assume things were going to improve. Melodie comes back into the room with Emma Beane behind her in skyscraper heels and a clingy jersey dress in baby pink.

"Emma, what a surprise!" Steve says.

"Hi, Steve. Melodie invited me and Daddy last night, but he forgot about a business meeting this morning, so he couldn't make it," she says with a grin that could be called impish...if you enjoy seeing barracudas smile. She spins around, then puts a hand over her chest with a gasp. "Matt! I didn't know you'd be here. Your mom didn't say."

Yeah, right. Everything just coincidentally aligned to help her out. Besides, last night? Why in the world would Melodie invite her last night...

Then I remember. Melodie said she was with a client... Zack Beane. He must be Emma's father. Olivia said Emma's family's a client.

My head throbs harder. I should've just told Matt I was too sick to come and asked him to play doctor— clean or dirty, whichever version he wanted. Now it's too late, and I'm stuck in this ostentatious hellhole until we can make a graceful exit.

26

It's amazing how long a brunch can last. Theoretically, it shouldn't take more than half an hour to shovel eggs, pancakes and bacon down our collective throats. But Matt's parents linger for almost two hours. They linger over their food. They linger over their coffee. They linger over conversation. Emma laughs at every word out of Steve's and Melodie's mouths, as though they were God's new gift to standup comedy. I'm ready to crawl into a hole because it's either that or drive a pair of ice picks through my ears so I don't have to hear her grating laugh.

My head is pounding so hard I can barely think. My stomach isn't thrilled either, since I was forced to eat a few bites of food. It's really hard to rearrange your chow for hours while people linger.

I excuse myself, ostensibly to freshen my makeup, but it's really to take a little break from the company.

Matt's great, of course, but everyone else is a bit much. I still can't decide what Melodie and Steve think of me, but it's obvious they like Emma from the way they smile and nod at her. But then who wouldn't? She's less beautiful than Google Images would have you believe, but she's still pretty, young and sophisticated. Okay, her laugh is annoying, but maybe that doesn't bother Melodie and Steve. There's no rationale for taste—I mean, some people want pet skunks.

The bathroom is blissfully quiet, but my head still throbs—a residual throb, undoubtedly. Maybe it's a sign that I'm about to start my period, but I know better. I never get a headache during this time of the month. Gritting my teeth, I run some cold water over the pulse points on my wrists, but it doesn't help much. What wouldn't I give for a hot bath with extra bubbles!

Home is screaming my name, but I don't know of a graceful way to get out of here. I don't want to ask Matt, in case he thinks I don't like his parents. He did say he loved his mother.

One more hour. After that, I'll tell Matt I have to go because I have an afternoon outing with the girls. If I must, I'll go shopping to cover my lie. God, I'll even repeat the run of hell with Sammi.

Girding my loins and pasting on a smile, I leave the bathroom and quietly make my way back to the dining room. Emma's voice is carrying into the hall, and my jaw tightens.

"Did you really have to go for a girl like *that*?"

Cuz a snob like you is better? I think cattily.

NADIA LEE

She continues, "If you really wanted, I could've given you the baby you need."

Wait. I stop. *Who needs a baby?*

"We would've had to be married first, but I'm not thinking marriage at the moment," Matt says dryly.

Baby...marriage... *What?*

Emma laughs like what Matt said is hilarious, except he wasn't joking.

The baby you need.

Then I remember how Emma hinted about Matt needing to marry soon when she crashed our lunch date at Pearl China. Was she trying to imply she's pregnant...?

No. She can't be, based on what I just heard. So what the hell is she talking about?

Steve adds, in the mildly indulgent tone of a teacher reminding an earlier lesson point to a lazy student, "No marriage and baby, no trust fund until you turn forty."

There's a trust fund?

"And who has the time to waste until they're forty?" Emma asks.

"Someone who doesn't need the money, obviously," Melodie says tartly.

Thank you, Melodie. Maybe she's not so bad after all...except who doesn't need money?

"Everyone needs money," Emma points out, as though she's read my mind around the corner and through a doorway. "Five million is a lot to sit on for years and years. Don't you agree, Matt?"

My jaw drops. *Five million dollars?* Matt is going to come into that much money if he's married and has a baby?

Oh my God. Why didn't this come up during Sammi's digging? Don't tell me this time she used a hand shovel. She normally uses an excavator.

Emma continues, "There's no guarantee that girl of yours is going to marry you, much less want to have your baby."

What the hell. Is she saying Matt's with me only for money?

Of course! He is too good for you. You know that, my mind whispers, and I swear the blood in my veins goes colder than ice.

"I've done the whole rodeo with marriage, and I'm willing to do it again plus have a kid or two with the right man."

I almost throw up in my mouth.

She suddenly gasps. "Unless you're trying to do it in reverse order—get her pregnant, then marry her."

Get her pregnant, then marry her.

The words pound into my head with such impact that I feel like my skull's exploding.

I've never provided my own condoms with Matt because I trusted him. And now my period's late. And coffee and food are making me feel bad.

Shit. I know enough about what happens when you get pregnant to be aware that nausea comes when a bun starts occupying the oven. I don't think what I've been experiencing is nausea per se, but it could be a very minor version...a cellular-sized version.

But I'm on the pill.

Which is only about ninety-one percent effective, according to the CDC's effectiveness with typical use statistics, my mind whispers. Just in case I'm not freaking out enough.

"Emma." Matt's voice is mildly chiding.

Is he annoyed because Emma called him on it? And how come Emma knows about this money thing, but I don't? She's his ex. I'm his girlfriend.

Aren't I?

"I know you've been spending money to help the family of that guy who keeled over at your old firm," Emma says. "There's no way your new company's paying you enough for that plus your living expenses."

"I helped raise money for his funeral, not to support his elderly parents for life."

Emma's voice grows shrill at Matt's explanation. "Do you really want to wait until you're forty to touch the money that's rightfully yours? Or get that unmotivated, lazy girl to marry you and give you a baby? You know if the mom's dumb, the babies are dumb too! I read an article about it. You deserve better than her! We'd make the smartest, most beautiful babies."

Blood crashes around in my head, roaring and frothing like storm waves against a cliff. I can't digest, I can't think. My purse strap slides down my arm, and I realize I'm shaking. I hug myself, suddenly chilled.

Going back into the dining room and confronting

everyone there seems...beyond me at the moment. They're acting and talking like I'm a means to an end—Matt getting his money. But that's ridiculous, isn't it? Stuff like that happens in books and movies. People don't actually try to get others pregnant or whatever for money anymore. Not people like Matt anyway. He's civilized. Educated. Sweet Darlings Inc. pays him well, I'm sure. He doesn't need the five million dollars.

But...

Why has he been so nice to me? So perfect? I'm not pretty like Emma, accomplished like my cousins, or sophisticated and well put together like so many people at the firm.

What I *am* is young, naïve and inexperienced. Is that why he targeted me? Because he could tell that about me at a glance? This may be a marathon, but our relationship milestones seem to be happening at a faster pace than usual. It only took him like a week to convince me to sleep with him. And if he'd just given us a few more weeks and asked me to marry him, I'd have said yes. If he'd asked me to have his baby, I'd have said yes to that too...

My heart thunders.

I've fallen for him. Hopelessly. Pathetically.

And realizing that right now is salt on a fresh, open wound.

I hear voices. They're talking, but garbled through the roar in my head. Spots swim in my vision. I have to get out of here before I start hyperventilating and lose it.

My hand clenched around my purse strap, I sneak out of the house. Nobody notices. Why should they? I'm nothing. Just a tool.

The early autumn air is refreshingly cool against my skin. I try to draw it in, but my lungs are too constricted. I plod several blocks before I realize I have no idea where I'm going. Even if I did, McLean is too far from Dulles to walk.

And logically it makes sense I get a ride. But not with Matt. He's probably busy. No. He *is* busy, no probably about it.

I call for Lyft. A car shows up in a few minutes, and I ask the driver to take me home, while he stares at me like I'm a black plague carrier.

He starts off after handing me a couple of Kleenex. Only then do I realize I've been crying.

The drive is quiet, which sucks because the words from earlier fill the silence.

I could've given you the baby you need.

Everyone needs money.

Five million.

I'm willing to do it again plus have a kid or two.

Get her pregnant, then marry her.

Matt never once told her to shut up. Does that mean he honestly considered getting me pregnant so he could play the hero and manipulate me into marrying him? Or that he's not at all opposed to marrying Emma and having a baby with her if I'm too much work?

God, I feel so stupid.

I tip the driver generously, since he didn't try to

chase after a cheating girlfriend or hit on me or anything crazy like that. And because he gave me more Kleenex so I could blow my nose and dry my face as well as possible. I look like shit in my compact mirror, but on a scale from one to ten—ten being *what the hell happened to you?*—I'm like a three, which means I can probably go in and blame my condition on the headache. The last thing I need is to alarm my house-mates. Or have them asking me questions.

As I step inside home, sweet home, my phone rings again. It's the fifth time. Or sixth. I don't remember. I lost count after the second time, and right now I have bigger things on my mind than giving a damn about who's calling, much less answering anything.

"Oh my God, you need to sit down," Sammi says.

Jesus. Do I still look *that* bad? "I have a headache," I mumble, stumbling across the hardwood floor and plopping down in an armchair. Then I notice something...

Sammi's pale. So is Michelle. An alarm goes off in my head.

"What's wrong?" I ask.

"You know the pharmacy where we get our prescriptions filled?"

"Yeah?"

"The manager there got arrested," Sammi says like it's the most horrible thing in the world. "We just saw the news."

I should probably look sufficiently curious. Maybe even drum up some concern. But right now, that man getting arrested is so inconsequential, I can't even. "Okay." I shrug.

"*It's not okay!*" Michelle screeches.

I wince. "Why not? What's the problem?"

"The reason he got arrested is he switched birth control pills with placebos!" Michelle is shaking, then places an unsteady hand on her forehead. "A whole bunch of women are pregnant because of him!"

Oh my God. *Oh my God!*

All my blood seems to drain from me. I'm so dizzy, I feel like my head is about to fly away like a balloon. No wonder my period changed after graduation. I wasn't on the pill at all.

"Tell me you've been careful," Sammi says.

"Condoms have a nineteen percent failure rate when you measure effectiveness in typical use." My voice is faraway and fleeting.

Michelle squints at me. "What?"

"That's what the CDC says." The pill I relied on is about as effective as water against pregnancy. If Matt wanted to get me pregnant...

I'm late.

I could be pregnant too. Just like my mom was with me.

Oh shit. Oh shit. *Oh shit.*

I jump to my feet, shove hands into my hair, clench my fingers until my scalp hurts.

Five million dollars. Money. Marriage. Baby.

Or wait until he's forty.

All the things I overheard jumble in my head until I

feel like I'm about to faint. What little food I had at Matt's parents' churns, and I run to the bathroom. I make it just in time.

Everything comes back up.

I wait until my breath settles and start to get up, but my belly isn't finished with me. I start heaving again, and it takes two more bouts before I'm really *finished* finished.

I think.

Sighing hard, I close my eyes and sit there, just in case. I need a pregnancy test ASAP. Maybe two. I'm sure they can tell by now. If I am pregnant...

Don't think about that.

I might not be pregnant. Maybe Matt didn't do anything. Maybe he is one of those rare people who really couldn't give a hoot about five million bucks. Or babies, or any of those things that get people really excited. I mean... Alexandra doesn't care that much about money, even when it's millions. But then she's worth at least a billion.

Matt isn't worth a billion, my mind reminds me, in case I forgot.

I feel a warm, soothing hand between my shoulder blades. "Hey, you all right?"

Every cell in my body tenses at Matt's voice. How the hell did he get inside?

On cue, he says, "Sammi let me in."

The knot in my belly tightens. I used to love it that he seemed to know exactly what I was thinking all the time.

Now I hate it. He can read me like a book. He can tell how pathetic, needy and naïve and stupid I am. And I resent my lack of sophistication—something all my cousins have. I may be Alexandra's granddaughter, but I'm nothing like the rest of my family.

I pull away, shrugging his hand off me. "What are you doing here?" My voice comes out in a croak. Wincing, I stand, ignoring his offer to help me up, and rinse out my mouth.

Stuffing his hands into his pants pockets, Matt watches me, his head tilted. "You were gone for a long time, so I went looking for you. When I couldn't find you I tried calling, then texted Sammi to see if she'd heard anything. She told me you'd come home looking like hell." His dark eyebrows pinch together. "Why didn't you say something?"

Speechless, I stare at him. Is he serious? When was I supposed to barge in? Before or after Emma offered to marry him and have his baby?

"Never mind. I should've known you weren't well enough for the visit. We should've cut it short."

"Right," I spit out. "Before Emma said she'd marry you and have your baby so you can get your money."

A small muscle near his left eyebrow twitches. "Jan..."

"Why didn't you tell me?"

"Because there's nothing between me and Emma. I was never going to marry her or have babies with her. We dated a few years ago, but were completely incompatible."

"She seems to disagree."

"Which has nothing to do with me."

"But what she said is true about the money, isn't it? You have five million dollars."

"Which is in a trust from my grandparents. I can't touch it anyway, and I don't plan on spending a penny of it."

"Why not? It's a lot of money."

"They left one for me and one for Olivia, so we'd never have to do work we don't believe in just to survive. But I don't need it because I'm making a good living doing exactly what I love doing. So my plan was to donate half of the trust to causes I believe in and give the other half to my kids in the future so they can have the same freedom I had. Trust me, Jan. You shouldn't worry about the money. It was never a factor in any of my life decisions."

Put that way, it's so logical. Too damn logical. Just like he's too damn perfect. "You really want me to believe the money had nothing to do with anything?" Before he has a chance to answer, I plow on because the fact that my period is late is drumming in my head. "You honestly never wanted me pregnant?"

The muscles in his jaw bunch together. Thoughts cross his gaze, but they're totally opaque. If I were the one thinking, Matt would know everything going through my mind. And that infuriates me more.

"Why can't you answer me?" I yell.

"Yes," he says, his voice entirely too calm. "I would

love to have that future with you—share a home, have children and grow old."

It's such a lovely vision—the kind I would've swooned over. And that is so damn unfair. He sounds like an adult while I'm like a lost, panicked child inside. My hands shake, sweat slickening my palms.

"But not unless that's what you want too," he adds.

"Right. The moment I walked through that door"— I point—"I learned the pill I've been taking is a placebo."

He takes a moment to process this, then frowns. "Well...okay. So? We used condoms."

"Yes. Ones you provided, and *my period's late.*" My voice rises to a screech.

His features freeze for a moment until sudden fury blazes in his eyes. The pulse in his now blotchy neck visibly throbs as he grates out, "*What the hell are you implying?*"

"What do you think?" I say, because I can't figure out what I'm trying to say. My stomach is churning again as though it wants to heave one more time, except there's nothing left. Uncontrollable emotions break over me, one after another, hitting me like perfectly executed punches until I'm barely standing. "You're too perfect, always knowing just what I need to hear and telling me exactly that. I should've known something was up when a guy like you pursued a girl like me."

"If that's what you thought, why the fuck did you come to my place, asking me to be your first?"

Because I was falling for you. "Because you were conveniently next door," I say instead. The truth is too humiliating.

He regards me for a moment, completely frozen. Then he turns so quickly I can barely follow and his fist connects with the wall, leaving a dent. The sudden bang stuns me, and I almost jump. His shoulders heave as he breathes in harshly, and a taut moment passes before he faces me again. His mouth tightens, then curls into a derisive line. "You're such a chickenshit."

It takes a moment before the insult registers. "How dare you."

"You're too damn blind to what others see in you— beautiful, smart, hard-working and vulnerable. You're so busy worrying about what little flaws you have that you can't appreciate the whole beauty of yourself."

"Shut up."

"*You* shut up. Even Michelangelo's *David* is flawed if you want to nitpick."

"I'm not Michelangelo or the *David*!" I yell out like an inane fool. But I can't process what he's saying, not really. Thoughts are spinning in my head like tornados, churning everything around, and it's all I can do to keep myself together.

"No, you're not!" He flings an arm out, then his hand tightens into a white-knuckled fist as he pounds his chest. "You're a woman I've fallen for, except you're too insecure to let this play out! You've been waiting for the other shoe to drop, for me to find a reason why I can't possibly love you!"

"You *don't* love me. You *like* things about me. You...you said..."

The look he gives me is sad. Disappointed. Why can't he be just angry? Why is he looking at me like I'm the one who failed us when he's the one who hid a five million-dollar secret? "I love everything about you. *I love you.* But I've been trying to give my heart to a woman who can't accept it. Won't accept it."

He's not making any sense. Why is he saying this now? I don't get it. "That's not true. You don't know enough about me. The money—"

He raises a finger in warning. "*Don't even go there!*"

And I shut my mouth because even though I'm barely rational, I can sense he's about to break.

"If I just wanted money," he hisses in a furious voice, "I would've definitely gotten you pregnant and married you, not because I'm greedy for the five million, but for *your* inheritance."

"What inheritance?"

He laughs, but it's mocking. Ugly. "You're one of Alexandra's heirs. You're due one fifth of her money because whatever your mother was going to get is going to go to you."

That can't be... He has to be wrong. He has to be wrong about everything. This is about *him* and *his* trust fund and *his* need to marry and have a baby and my period being late... "Why would she... No way."

"Like I said, you just won't accept how others see you or feel about you." He shakes his head. For some reason, he looks heartbreakingly sad. Like one of Shakespeare's tragic heroes. Or maybe it is my heart that's breaking. "What a waste."

A sense of impending doom prickles over my skin. I know I can stop this—somehow—if I can just... I don't know what, but I know I could make the horrible sensation go away if I—just... "Don't make this about me," I blurt out.

He inhales deeply and slowly. "*I'm* not making it anything. It's a hundred percent about you."

He's withdrawing, reining in the anger and disillusionment—I can see it as though those emotions are color-coded in a bright neon red and funereal black. They're both inside him, festering. Seething. Just because the air around him isn't pulsing with light doesn't mean things are okay.

My mouth dries. "We aren't finished," I say. "You still have a lot to explain." Except I think he's said everything he wanted to, even if I haven't processed much of it. But he has to explain...and convince me...to what? I don't know what outcome I want, but this... This is killing me.

"Yes, we are. I have nothing more to say to you, Jan." He takes a step back. And it hurts, like I'm being sliced into ribbons.

But I can't stop him either. So I watch him walk out...every step a shard digging into my heart.

When the door closes behind him, my knees buckle.

27

"Y ou need to get up if you plan to be at work on time," Sammi says from my bedroom door. Her voice is hushed and careful, as though she's confronting some feral animal.

Yeah. That's me, an uncivilized, brutish creature on a bed, sheets tangled around her. Bet I look wild too. I haven't showered since Matt walked out on Saturday, and I sweated like a pig while shivering on Sunday even though all I did was lie in bed. I can feel the sticky layers of old perspiration clinging to my now cool skin.

"You really should." Michelle comes in and takes away the untouched lo mein she left on my desk yesterday. "You can't waste away over a man. I forbid it."

I wave them off, which takes considerably more effort than I'd like. They look at each other, and I read their unspoken communication loud and clear.

Sammi signals, *She's so out of it.*

One of Michelle's eyebrows rises. *What do we do?*

I don't know. Call her in sick?

Michelle's jaw firms. *I'll handle it.* "I'll have HR mark you as being sick."

See?

"But you really should pull yourself together," she adds.

My voice is listless. "Yeah yeah." I wish I could read Matt the way I can my housemates. Then none of this would've happened. Maybe I should start dating Sammi and Michelle. We could start a three-way lesbian commune. I'm sure they'd be okay with it. They're open-minded, one of the reasons we get along so well.

Sammi and Michelle go to work because they're well-adjusted individuals who can adult better than I can. I'm like...a mess. But then I knew that. I just didn't realize how much it would hurt when Matt realized it too.

Next time, I'm not dating a smooth-talking lawyer. Actually I'm not dating anybody. Fuck it. I'll be a nun. I'm not picky like Sammi. I don't need free Wi-Fi as long as the beds are comfortable and the clothes are clean. I'm sure nunneries have washing machines, but if not, I'll buy one for the abbey. It's going to be a charming little place in Austria. Once I get over Matt, I'll run up one of the hills nearby and sing every day (as long as I'm alone; I don't want to get deported for torturing the locals). Except I won't be meeting Captain von Trapp. No. I'll be the good sister who doesn't climb trees, or scrape her knees, or waltz around with curlers in her hair *and* always shows up for mass on time. The Mother Abbess will keep me because I'll be a perfect angel—a model nun.

Nobody here will miss me, except for Sammi and Michelle, and they can come visit. It'll give them a reason to fly to Europe. They've both said they want to go.

Time passes slowly, but I don't mind. It's not like I have anything to do, or any place to be. It's sort of nice to accept that I was right about a lot of things about me... Why did I struggle so hard to fit in? It seems silly now.

That evening, Sammi and Michelle check up on me. Michelle sighs. "You need to answer your phone. David asked me if you were all right when you didn't answer his calls or texts."

"He should've called Sammi," I say. "She would've been happy to talk to him."

Sammi sighs with exasperation. "That's so not the point."

"Then what is?"

"I went to the fourteenth floor."

I frown. "Did you tell David I wasn't coming in?"

"No," Sammi says. "I went by to check on Matt."

I glare at her. "You shouldn't have."

"We had a meeting between the app dev team and the finance team, and he happened to drop by briefly. If it makes you feel better, he looked like shit, so you guys are a perfect matching pair. Although if I have to be honest, he looked better than you since he was at least groomed and in a work-appropriate suit."

I swallow. "Good for him." Really. What else is there to say?

"God. You're so fucking *dense!*" Sammi yells, then leaves, stomping her feet.

Michelle clears her throat. "Don't mind her. She's under a lot of stress."

"I bet."

"You really should eat something. And drink some water. It'd be awful if you ended up in the hospital for malnutrition and dehydration."

I scoff. "Nobody goes to a hospital for that. This is America, the wealthiest and most powerful nation in the world," I say, although I don't know what that has anything to do with hospitalization for malnourishment and dehydration.

But I drink the water she leaves in my room because... Well. I'm thirsty, and maybe she's right about dehydration.

Of course drinking water has annoying consequences. When my bladder won't let me stay in bed anymore, I drag myself out and go to the bathroom. *Huh. I'm starting my period.*

I wait...

Three...

Two...

One...

Nope. Relief doesn't come flooding through me. The only thing I feel is cold indifference... Then slowly, like the tide, grief comes in to lap at me. It's nothing crippling—I already experienced that when Matt walked out. This is different—gentler, in a way, but no less painful. It eats away at me little by little, like a weak acid...but acid nonetheless.

If I let it, it'll eventually consume all of me.

But somehow doing something about it feels too monumental, too daunting a task.

So I return to bed and pull the sheets around me, tucking myself in because nobody else is going to.

28

By Wednesday, my housemates stop asking if I'm getting up to go to work. I haven't eaten since Saturday, but I'm not hungry. Most likely I have enough fat storage to hibernate for a few weeks.

But Sammi hasn't given up on reporting to me about how Matt's doing. Finally, I say, "I thought you were busy in app dev. Don't you have to wrap up the new feature to be launched before Christmas?"

"Yeah, but I can multitask," Sammi says. "He was in a navy pinstripe suit. It looked new. Maybe he went shopping. Extra cleanly shaved too. And a blonde came by the office to see him. They lunched together."

A nasty pit forms in my gut, but it's probably nothing. Olivia's blonde. "The one from Carlos's?"

"No. Emma Beane."

I almost gasp at the searing pain. He wasted no time. They're probably going to marry and have a baby.

For all I know, they might've already started a baby registry. Now I almost resent my period. *If I were pregnant...*

Ugh. What the hell am I thinking? That's the stupidest reason to want to be pregnant. Didn't I decide to be Maria at an Austrian abbey? The Vatican must take applications over the Internet by now. I should apply for an open nun position online rather than sitting here wishing I were pregnant with Matt's baby. Besides, do I want to have a child in this kind of situation? It seems pretty stupid. I don't want to end up like my mom, running around with a kid nobody really cares for.

I firm my quivering mouth and look away.

"Anyway... Want to know the rest?" Sammi says. If I didn't know any better, I'd say she sounds gleeful. *What the hell?* She's my best friend. She's supposed to be mad on my behalf!

"*No!* Say one more word, and I'm evicting your ass!" I snarl, then pull the sheet over my head.

Sammi gets the hint. She isn't a total idiot.

Michelle, who's apparently heard my outburst, comes in—I can hear her through the sheet—and says, "Ignore Sammi. She's antsy and upset that she doesn't know how to fix this for you."

Maybe. Sammi *is* a fixer...

"For your information, Matt looks like shit these days."

"He has a new suit. Cleanly shaven. Dating Emma now," I say through the sheet.

"The suit is probably not new. All his legal eagle suits look the same. And lunch is not a date. So what if he's clean-shaven? His complexion is crap. I bet you he isn't getting more than four hours of sleep a night."

I take a tiny comfort over the news, since Michelle knows stuff like this. Then my insidious mind suggests maybe he isn't getting much sleep because he's too busy fucking Emma, and I want to sink into the earth and never come out again.

My aimless existence changes on Friday, though.

At around nine thirty, knocks come from the door. I ignore them. I'm not interested in salesmen or Jehovah's Witnesses. I'm sure the latter doesn't offer paid nunships to young women.

Besides, why should I get up? They'll go away soon enough.

I turn over and pull the sheet over my head, then sigh when it rises over my feet. I hate it when my feet aren't covered.

"Good Lord, Jan."

What?

I blink, then push the sheet off my face and sit up. I'm definitely not hallucinating. It's Alexandra. In my bedroom. She's dressed for work in a sweater dress and cute flats. A sizable thermos hangs from her shoulder.

"Grandma... What are you doing here?" My voice is rusty and croaky. Damn it. I reach for the bottle of water Michelle left by my bed.

"When David said you were out sick again, I had to stop by."

I take a swallow of the water, then say, "But it's nine thirty. Don't you have an important meeting or something?"

She looks impatient. "Nothing's more important than making sure you're all right. You weren't answering your phone."

"Oh." I clear my throat. "Sorry. I'm okay. Really."

"Then why have you lost weight?" She comes over and places a hand on my forehead. "No fever, at least. You look absolutely wretched. Have you eaten anything? Michelle said you didn't have much appetite."

"Did she come by to see you?" If so, that's just wrong. Friends don't rat friends out.

"No, I dropped by her desk. Wait right here."

She vanishes, leaving the thermos by my bed. I sigh. Guess she wanted to make sure I was still alive, but she shouldn't have bothered. I'm a human cockroach that can survive anything, including a nuclear holocaust...which is what the breakup with Matt seems like. I feel utterly gross—understandable, if I'm really a cockroach—and I probably smell as bad as I feel. I haven't showered since Saturday. The mirror in the bathroom shows how pathetic I am every time I walk by because the human body is a strange thing. Even though I'm not drinking much water, it still wants me to pee. You'd think that it'd want to hold onto every drop, right?

At least my period ended early yesterday evening. It's like the universe is saying, *Hey girl, I know your life's become a total fuckstorm, so how about this to make up for it?*

Yeah. Some consolation prize.

Alexandra returns soon with a bowl and a spoon. She opens the thermos and pours a small portion of chicken noodle soup into the bowl. "Here. Have some."

I look at it, then take a spoonful. It tastes just like Mom's, and a sudden longing and sadness spiral from a deep corner of my heart. To disguise the surge of silly emotions, I say, "This is good. Did Mrs. Jones make it?" That's Alexandra's housekeeper.

"No. It's my mother's recipe. I made it last night after I came home."

I stare at her open-mouthed. "You shouldn't have."

"I'm your grandmother. It's my job to take care of you."

Right. Obligation because we're family.

"Go on. Finish it up."

And I do because that's what granddaughters are supposed to do when their grandmothers bring home-made chicken noodle soup. I must admit, having warm food in my belly makes me feel almost human. "What's going on, Jan?" Alexandra asks me when I'm done. "You've never been sick or taken time off from anything without good reason."

"I have a very good reason, Grandma." I sigh, and my entire body collapses like a marionette with its strings cut. To my horror, tears prickle my eyes, and I drop my gaze, turning my head away.

She scoots over, taking the spot right next to me at

the edge of the mattress and puts an arm around my shoulders even though I have to be stinkier than a dog that's been rolling in dead fish. But it doesn't seem to bother her.

"Come on," she says. "Tell me."

"David said he put me up for a marketing analyst promotion, but I don't want it," I blurt out the least of my worries because I don't know how to start with the big one. Baby steps, baby steps.

She blinks. "Then you don't have to be a marketing analyst."

"I also don't want to go to San Mateo."

"Then you don't have to go there either."

"But you said..."

"I know what I said, but I didn't realize you were so unhappy about it."

"But you want me gone...don't you?"

Alexandra turns my head so we're eye-to-eye. "Want you *gone*? Have you lost your mind?"

"Why else would you ask me to move there? Nobody from the family's working in San Mateo."

"Sweetie, I only brought it up as something you should consider. Lots of people on the app dev team want to be in the Bay Area. I didn't realize you thought I was trying to get rid of you. Why would you think that?"

"Because..." I sigh. "I'm a mess. I know I've disappointed you all my life."

A variety of expressions crosses her concerned face, but I can't make out what she's thinking. But then, she didn't end up leading a very successful privately held app company by being an open book.

The silence is unbearable, so I keep going. "I can't dance. I can't sing. I know you were shocked when I got accepted to UVA. I was too. I didn't think I'd get in, and actually considered getting an associate's degree instead, and—"

"Jan, stop." She squeezes my hand tightly. "Just stop for a moment. The only reason why you don't dance well is because you inherited your mother's coordination, or lack thereof. She was a terrible dancer, except she liked it anyway, so she did it, not caring what others thought. And if you ever heard your mom sing, you would've considered it cruel and unusual punishment. As for my shock, I was stunned you applied in the first place. I didn't think you would because you're always so hard on yourself. I'd resigned myself to sending you to a school far beneath your true abilities. You don't understand how happy I was when you decided to attend UVA. I'm even starting a scholarship in your name at Comm School next year."

"Really?"

"Sweetie, you're so self-critical, it's painful for me to watch. You're such a perfectionist and can't accept any flaws in yourself, even though you're forgiving of others. Nobody's perfect, even if they appear that way. Do you know your uncle Dan took cooking lessons for a year to prepare a gourmet dinner for his wife on their anniversary, but it was so awful they went out to eat instead?"

I stare at her. Uncle Dan is probably the most aggressive grill hoarder every time we have a family cookout. He's the first to run to it and always argues with his brothers about who should do what.

"And Josh still can't ski well, even though he pretends he's a master skier and shares ridiculous selfies all the time." She rolls her eyes.

If I weren't so stunned, I'd roll my eyes too. My oldest cousin, Josh, always acts like the only reason why he didn't compete in the Olympics is because he didn't have the interest.

"And I'll tell you something I've never told anybody," Alexandra says.

"Okay."

"I'm sure you've noticed I never show my teeth when I smile."

I nod.

"I have a crooked upper tooth and a small gap between my two front teeth, and I'm so self-conscious that I just can't smile like most people."

"No way."

"It's true." She inhales, then pulls her lips back in a smile, showing me exactly what she's talking about.

Shamelessly, I peer at the teeth. They don't look terrible. The "defects" she's worried about are hardly even noticeable.

"See?" she says. "Hideous."

"You have got to be joking."

She snorts.

I pull back and look at her. "If they bother you that much, why don't you do something about them?"

"Because." She sighs. "My family couldn't afford braces when I was little, and by the time I felt I could afford them, I was in my thirties, much too old for such things. They're for kids—teenagers. So I'm stuck with teeth that make me self-conscious enough to affect the way I smile..." She shakes her head ruefully. "You see how silly this whole situation is."

I give her a small grin. "But you're still awesome, still Alexandra Darling. I'm..." I brace myself. "What if I'm really, truly, fundamentally...flawed?"

"What do you mean?"

"You didn't approve of my dad. And Mom never really talked about him much. What if... What if he's somebody terrible? I mean, he could be in jail this very minute."

Alexandra's face crumbles, and she reaches out and holds my hand. "Jan, no. Your father... He was a good man."

"You don't have to make up lies." I look down at my hands. "Even Mom was ashamed of him at the end. She put down 'John Doe' for 'Father' on my birth certificate."

"But that was his name."

My head snaps up. "What?"

"Didn't you know? He was an orphan, and nobody bothered to give him a real name, so he got stuck with John Doe. He didn't care enough to change it."

"But you disapproved of him. Why, if he's such a

good guy?" Then something else strikes me. "Is he dead?"

Alexandra nods. "Six months after you were born." She sighs. "Let me tell you from the beginning, so you can understand all this." Her hand tightens around mine. "When he started dating Mer, I *didn't* think highly of him. He was a good-looking, smooth-talking young man. I hate to say this, but I had my own prejudices, and didn't find him good enough for my only girl. But Mer was crazy about him. When I told her to stay away from him, she argued. I said he was beneath her, and she called me an arrogant old bat. She spoke of having his children, and that's when I told her no child of John Doe would ever be considered my grandchild. She must've known that I would never change my mind, so she ran off with him. Then she had you. He did his best to provide for her and you, working two jobs. He died half a year later. 'A simple robbery gone wrong' is what I was told. He was working a second job in an unsafe part of town to provide for you and your mother." Alexandra takes a moment to inhale shakily. "It's my deepest regret that I wasn't there for any of you. I should've been. You're my family, and I love you."

I sniff. Alexandra reaches over and swipes my cheeks with her fingers, and I realize I've been crying.

"It hurts me to see you not realize how lovely you are. You're a miracle child, Jan. I'm not sure if you read your mom's journals, but she almost lost you. But even without reading them, I knew you were something truly special when I learned your name was Jan."

"How?"

"Because Jan was the nickname your grandfather used to call me." She gives me a tremulous smile. "Bernie thought Alexandra was too formal a name and decided to call me Jan, short for January, which is my middle name. It was fitting, too—we met in January and married exactly a year later. So when I heard your name, I knew Mer was reminding me you were my granddaughter, and she was also telling me she forgave me for my harsh words. And every day I regret not having looked her up and reached out, instead of hoping she'd realize the error of her ways and come crawling back. I should've never been so arrogant. If I hadn't, I might still have my daughter and son-in-law. And you might have your parents." Her eyes are red-rimmed. "I'm so sorry, Jan."

My arms wrap around her, and we hold each other, our tears mingling. My self-doubts and insecurity seem to melt with every drop we shed, and I wish I hadn't been such an idiot—making assumptions about myself. Then I wouldn't have wasted so much time and energy.

Eventually, we pull away, and she dries my face. "Feel better now?"

I nod. Then because she's been honest, unflinchingly so, I tell her, "I'm dating Matt Aston."

"I know," she says.

"You do?" Grandma's NSA strikes again.

"He came by to see me last week. He wanted to let me know and ask for my blessing."

"He did?"

"I suspect he isn't the type to indulge in interoffice dating, but since it's happening and you're my grand-daughter, he wanted to make sure. Good thing he did, too, because I told him I wouldn't tolerate any kind of fortune hunting."

"Fortune hunting?" I choke out.

"Your inheritance," she says, as if it's the most obvious thing in the world.

So Matt wasn't just saying it. I *am* an heiress. I had no idea.

Because you don't care about money and never once believed Alexandra would leave anything to you.

I didn't think I deserved anything.

"I also warned him about breaking your heart," she says coldly. Her eyes glint in a way I've never seen before. It's a good thing the look wasn't directed at me, or I might've peed in my pants. "Now tell me. Is he the real reason you've been neglecting yourself?"

"Uh. No. Well... It's complicated."

"Don't overanalyze. Either tell him to make it right or he can prepare to resign."

"Grandma!"

"Don't you *grandma* me. I can forgive almost anything except you being hurt. I'm not going to tell you who to date. I've already paid a heavy price for that sort of arrogance. But I won't let you suffer because some idiot can't figure out how to make his woman happy."

My jaw drops. "Matt is a Harvard-educated lawyer."

"I don't care where he got his fancy degree," she scoffs. "A man who can't make his woman happy is an idiot as far as I'm concerned."

"Yes, Grandma," I say meekly.

"Now. You'll shower, and eat all the soup I brought you, and take the rest of the day to pull yourself together. Then you'll join me and the family for your birthday celebration on Saturday."

"My birthday?"

"Yes. It's today. You forgot again, didn't you?"

"Yeah." I've never bothered to remember. It never felt important, even though Alexandra made sure to throw a bash every year.

"And starting next week, I expect you to resume your regular life. Living well is the best revenge. Nobody is worth neglecting yourself for. And don't forget, you always have me on your side." She gives me a tight hug. "Now I have to get back to work. Call me if you need anything, and if David bothers you, tell *him* to call me."

"Okay."

She leaves. I have another bowl of the soup, then shower, scrubbing my body with extra care. I even wash my hair twice to make sure I'm as clean as I can be. Since my clothes and sheets smell rank, I toss them all into the washer.

Then I slowly make my way down to the garage. I reach into the back and drag out the boxes of Mom's things. They're tightly duct-taped—four layers—to make sure nothing can spill out by accident. I pull at them, then give up and go to the kitchen for a paring knife.

With care, I cut the tape and open the first box. I find Mom's journals. They're old, the pages wrinkled in places where water somehow got to them. I pick up the first one and start reading.

Every entry is thoughtful, full of her inner dialog, almost too raw and honest for me to read without tearing up. But through them all, one thing's clear. She loved my dad. She adored me. She never talked much about him because it hurt too much. She longed to reconcile with Alexandra, but she didn't know how to do it because she was afraid I might be rejected, and the last thing she wanted was for me to feel unwanted. She chose to be on her own, cut off from the family and relatives she missed, than have me be rebuffed.

I dab at my eyes and blow my nose. It's amazing how your perspective on life changes when you realize how wrong and blind you've been...

I've been loved all my life. Protected. Cherished.

And I've been the biggest damn idiot for not realizing that because I didn't feel like I measured up to others. And look at me, wasting an entire week because I'm a self-indulgent fool.

It's almost four now.

I get up and check my phone. It's out of charge.

After I plug it in for a while, messages download. David called me seven times, texted me fifteen. The last one came earlier today.

–David: Hope you're okay. Take care of yourself.

My work email is bursting with new messages. The latest is from Tim from app dev. He wants to chat with me about the opening I applied for. My mouth dries, and I take a few deep breaths to slow down my unsteady pulse and wipe the sweat from my palms. The me from before would've responded by freaking out, then sabotaged it by telling myself I wasn't good enough and Tim was only doing this because Alexandra asked him to or because he wanted to ingratiate himself with her. But not now. I know he's doing this because he liked my application and thought I'd be a good fit. I type "Sure, what time's good for you?" and hit send.

Then I scroll through for anything from Matt, but he hasn't sent me a single text. Not a call. Nothing.

But then why would he? He made it very clear we were finished when he walked out on Saturday. I look out the window. He's still at work, of course. It's only four in the afternoon.

Matt's right. I work hard. I'm not an idiot—Tim liked my comment at the meeting. Given his reputation, it's highly unlikely he was just saying it to be nice. And David likes my work performance well enough to put me up for a promotion early. Did I screw up everything with my insecurity? Have I pushed away the most perfect man for me? Part of me wants to head over to

Sweet Darlings Inc. and talk to him, but I can't. Not right now. I have to get my head screwed on right first.

I don't give a shit if Emma's circling Matt like some starving vulture. I'm worthy of the man who told me he loved me...because I love him back just as much, and I'm smart enough—and finally brave enough—to fight for us.

29

By the time I'm in my favorite blue sunflower dress and wedge heels, it's starting to rain. I go downstairs to wait for Matt's BMW to show and frown at four vases of fresh flowers—red roses and orchids. Huh. Wonder who they're for. They are not Sammi's thing, and Michelle isn't dating seriously at the moment.

I'm super tense, so I hit the massage chair, hoping time will pass a little quicker. It's almost five thirty now. Matt should be coming home soon. Hopefully nobody's doing a deal or having a meeting in another time zone that'll require him to work late.

Sammi walks through the door. "Oh my God, are you... Is this really Jan?"

"Har har. Yes. It's me."

"Thank God." She puts a hand over her chest. "I was worried about you, girl. Thought about going for reinforcements."

"I know. Sorry."

"So why are you up? Bed sores?"

"Alexandra came by."

"Oh." Sammi's eyebrows rise, although it doesn't quite disguise her wince. "Hope it wasn't too painful."

"No ass kicking. She helped me see things more clearly."

"Good. In fact, great."

"Sorry I've been such an idiot all this time."

"No, no, stop! It's my duty as your friend to stand by you no matter what."

See? This is why I love my friends.

"So why are you all dolled up?" She brightens. "Wanna go out?"

"Sorry. I'm actually...waiting to settle things with Matt."

"Reconciliation or..." She runs a finger across her neck.

"Making up."

As she's about to say something, Michelle walks in. "Ugh. Fuck this stupid rain," she mutters under her breath.

And I know she's on her period without her having to say it. She never talks like that except when Aunt Flo is visiting, and rain aggravates her cramps. Suddenly she stops when she notices me. "Oh my gosh. You're out of bed. Was there a fire?"

I laugh softly. I can't help it. It's sort of funny how both my friends are shocked. On the other hand, it probably means I was in a worse place than I realized.

"This calls for a celebration," Michelle says. "Let's go out and *I'm* buying *you*"—she looks at me meaningfully—"a drink."

"Actually, I can't."

"She's going to go over to Matt's to make things all smoochy again."

Michelle blinks. "You sure that's the right move?"

Cold sweat slickens my palms. *Does she know something I don't?* "Why?"

"It's always best if you have the guy come to you first. Better leverage."

"He already told me he loved me."

Michelle purses her lips. "Mmm... But he still stayed away. That's not good."

Sammi nods behind Michelle.

"What if he never comes?" I ask.

"He will." Sammi's tone's entirely too confident. And it makes me worry because her track record isn't the best when it comes to stuff like this.

"How do you know?"

"After I saw him with Emma Beane, I might possibly have very casually mentioned that you joined a dating site or two." She shrugs.

"Oh my God." I cover my face, my shoulders shaking with suppressed laughter. At least I think I'm laughing, because I'm not crying.

"I didn't want him thinking you were pining over him."

"He already knows. I haven't been to work in a week!"

"Ha! Bow to my genius, because he's not thinking that at all."

Oh no...

Sammi rubs her hands. "He's convinced that you're hunting for another guy. I told him you've realized that falling for the first guy you had sex with is a limiting proposition because you haven't explored the field widely enough to be certain. And to make sure he *viscerally* grasps that you are legit one of the most sought-after babes in town, not only did I have you join a bunch of dating sites, but I also set it up so that Matt gets CC'd every time a potential suitor messages you." She beams and waits, like a cat waiting to be praised after bringing home a dead rodent.

I know she means well. And she really wants to help, and I love her dearly for that. But this... I shake my head.

"What? You got over a hundred interests!"

My jaw drops. "Over a hundred?"

She nods. "I Photoshopped your pic a little. You know, added a cup size, gave you that slightly fun, slutty look. Plus I'm great at writing ad copy for that kind of thing."

Ad copy. As though I'm for sale on eBay. *Slightly used former virgin, sold as-is, the image is for marketing purposes only and may not reflect the actual merchandise.*

Michelle nods. "A great move. Any day now, Matt will cave and come over."

"Exactly. And I've studiously avoided him since

then to ensure he's dying of curiosity. Plus, I had random bouquets of flowers delivered to the house, so he can see you're being courted."

"Courted..." I pinch the bridge of my nose. So that explains the flowers.

"Yup."

"Wait a couple of days," Michelle says. "If he still doesn't come over, then you can decide what to do."

I stand up, raising both hands, palms out. "Sammi, Michelle, I love you guys, but you have to stop. This is my life." I straighten my spine. "I'm not waiting anymore."

30

In the end, I turn down Michelle's offer to redo my makeup and go straight to Matt's place. If it had been even a day earlier, I would've taken her up on it. However, makeup has nothing to do with my confidence or how people perceive me (so long as I don't look like a slob). And I know it has no impact on how Matt feels about me.

As I'm about to leave, somebody knocks on my door. Wait. Are Sammi and Michelle correct? Is that Matt?

My heart hammering, I open the door, then almost let out an "Ew" when I see Emma standing there. She's carefully outfitted in a ridiculously ostentatious designer dress that matches her hot pink umbrella. A few raindrops cling to her snake-skin ankle boots, and she looks at me like I'm the most loathsome thing she's ever seen.

Which doesn't bother me, since the feeling is mutual.

"What do you want? Matt's house is over there," I say, then I almost smack myself. Ugh. *What the hell?* It's like I'm encouraging her to go bang him or something.

"I know where he lives," she says between clenched teeth. "I'm here to say I'm sorry for being less than polite to you."

I blink at the most incongruously delivered apology. Her expression is more suited for "Fuck you, bitch." A vein in her forehead is visibly throbbing. I wonder if it's going to pop.

She draws in a deep breath. "I shouldn't have interrupted your date with Matt or insinuate that he's only using you to have a baby. And...*stuff*."

Except her eyes are saying she did nothing wrong. What the hell is going on?

"Anyway, I said I'm sorry, so don't you dare claim I didn't." Before I can gather my wits, she spins around, jumps into her sports car and vanishes.

What was that about?

I shake myself mentally. *Who cares about Emma? She isn't important.* Matt is.

My hand is slick around the umbrella handle as I go over to his house, and it has nothing to do with rain. Although I had a glass of water before leaving, my mouth is so dry it's painful. I clear my throat and knock on the door.

Before my knuckles hit for the third time, the door swings open, and Matt is standing on the other side, silently studying me. Something like worry darkens his gaze before it turns guarded, without the usual sparkle.

He seems a bit leaner—maybe it's the light—and there are half-circles under his eyes. Michelle said he probably wasn't sleeping much, but he still looks scrumptious in a charcoal suit. His tie is missing, the collar undone. If this had been back before we fought, I might've stretched myself up and kissed the bare skin at the base of his throat.

But right now, his expression is inscrutable, his mouth flat. If he's surprised to see me at his doorstep, I can't tell. For all I know, I could've imagined he was concerned for me because I really *really* want him back.

My heart pounds.

"Uh. Is it okay if I come in? It's raining pretty hard." The second the inane words leave me lips, I wince. I have an umbrella. I can just run back to my place next door. Shoulda brought an empty bowl for sugar or something. That way it would be less lame.

Matt's going to roll his eyes and shut the door in my face in...

Three...

Two...

"Come in." He steps aside.

"Okay. Sorry to—" I stop. Did he just say, "Come in?"

He arches an eyebrow.

Oh. Yes. Yes, he did.

My heart beats faster. *Breathe.* Can you imagine the spectacle if I hyperventilated and passed out at his feet? Ugh. I might as well just give up.

No. No negative thoughts. No giving up.

I'm worthy. I'm lovable. And people do love me.

I just have to convince this man that *we* are still worth fighting for, that we can have the future he spoke of.

The door closes behind me with a soft click. "There are things I have to say. That's why I really came in, not just because it's raining," I say.

"Okay."

"So. Um. I was thinking about what happened, and it's..." God, this is so hard. I wish I could read Matt's mind, but his expression seems even more remote than before. Crap. I stop pacing because my knees are so squishy and shaky that there's no way I can take another step without landing on my ass. "I shouldn't have done that. Accused you that way, I mean. And in case you're wondering, I'm not pregnant."

He shoves his hands into his pants pockets. "Is that why you're here?"

"Um... I thought you should know." I clear my throat. Why isn't he happy? Did he want the hypothetical baby? Aren't we too young for it? "And you were —*are* right about my insecurities. I'm not really like other people."

"Jan—"

I raise a sweaty hand. "Let me finish." I tell him about my childhood, things I've never told anybody, then more recent stuff, including Alexandra's offer to move me to San Mateo. "I want you to know the first thing I thought was *San Mateo doesn't have Matt.*" I peer at him through my lashes. A fleeting smile on his lips gives me the courage to plow on. "You're the one who made me realize—unconsciously—that I was giving my past too much power over me. If I hadn't met you, I'd probably be on my sixth or seventh one-night stand and Baileying on the guy because I wouldn't be able to go through with it...all the while wondering what's wrong with me. I've been telling myself I liked you, that I was insanely fond of you, but really I've been in love with you all along but didn't want to admit it because I was afraid of what it might mean if I did. What if you didn't love me back? What if you thought I wasn't good enough? Maybe that's why I wanted you to remain as just That Man Next Door, rather than someone who could mean more."

Amazement glitters in his warm gaze. "Jan, you're so damn fucking perfect, I don't understand how you can't see that. But if you give me a chance, I'll help you see yourself through my eyes."

Something like hope sparks in my heart. "So...we're not finished...?"

"Finished? Are you kidding? It's been hellish without you, and I was thinking of ways I could fix it after the debacle last Saturday. In case you heard the worst possible interpretation from your nosy house-mates, I met with Emma and told her she needed to stop deluding herself."

"What do you mean?"

"Thinking that we can be together if she just pesters me long enough, because I feel absolutely nothing for her. And she's supposed to apologize to you before the week's over. Let me know if she doesn't. I also told Mom I wasn't joining Aston Richter Spencer Emerick even if you weren't in the picture, so she needs to stop trying to manipulate me, including sending me ugly housewarming gifts to express her displeasure."

"Wow."

"Yeah. And if you'd waited just a few more minutes, you would've found me on *your* doorstep, asking you to come over because I had something for your birthday. Then once you had, I would've convinced you to give us another chance...because I shouldn't have walked out on you like that when you were in shock and felt betrayed. Or, if that failed, I was willing to seduce you into staying with me."

I finally register a cake and a pile of presents wrapped in sunflower paper on the dining table. Sweet bliss unfurls in my heart, chasing away the cold and misery of the last six days. I sway closer until I'm only a hairsbreadth away from him. "You knew?"

He pulls his hands out of his pockets and locks them at the small of my back, cinching us together. "David mentioned it. You have no idea how lucky I felt for that small pretext to see you again, because I was becoming increasingly irrational about you. It didn't help that your witchy friend kept telling me about your potential dates, and all those guys' messages kept landing in my inbox."

"You know that wasn't really me who signed up." I wrap my arms around him.

"Yeah...but I was jealous anyway."

"How could you be, when you're the only man I love?"

He runs the back of his fingers along my cheek. "Because I'm a possessive guy, and I'm utterly and insanely in love with you."

I bite my lower lip, trying not to smile too widely, but it's impossible.

Matt continues, "I don't want you near any man who wants you that way."

"What would you have done? Sued them? Slapped them with depositions?"

"No. I would've tackled them and held their faces to the ground until they begged for mercy."

"I thought you were a quarterback."

"I can still tackle better than most."

"I think you can do everything well."

"I can do everything well when it comes to you."

I look deeply into his warm blue eyes. "So. Are we good now?"

"Better than good. So what do you want to do first? Unwrap your gifts or eat your cake?"

"I'm definitely unwrapping my gifts first, and I'm

starting with the best one." I reach for his jacket, then slide it down over his arms.

With a wicked laugh, Matt picks me up and carries me to the bedroom.

The cake and gifts stay forgotten for a long, long time.

EPILOGUE: MATT

Sometimes it's a small and innocuous thing that opens the most important chapter of your life.

That night I met Jan, I was going to finish my martini at the midtown bar, go back to my hotel—my lease had expired a day earlier—and get a good night's sleep. Kind of lame, sure, but what's a guy to do when the friends who were supposed to send him off got stuck at work indefinitely?

Then Jan walked in.

And that was the moment that bisected my life—before Jan and after Jan.

I was leaving for Virginia the next day, but I wanted her so badly that I took her to my hotel room, telling myself I could get her number and call and come up for visits regularly. As long distance goes, northern Virginia to New York isn't too bad.

When her phone rang with a family emergency, interrupting us, I finally realized how selfish I was being. Long-distance relationships suck, and they never really work, especially for a new couple. All the associates at the firm who had girlfriends in areas outside the tri-state broke up within six months.

Besides, she wasn't like the other hard-nosed "I know what I want" associates I'd slept with. They had their lives mapped out, and I was only a tiny blip. But with Jan... I could see myself being an important chapter, just as I could see the same for her. She had an air of sweet vulnerability that said she was the type you called afterward, and took to dinner and movies and shows. She was going to find a nice guy in Brooklyn who'd do all those things with her someday, although the idea was oddly disturbing. But it was only fair I didn't go after her, knowing I wasn't going to stick around.

You cannot understand how much I thanked God and Buddha and every deity ever—even Zeus—when Jan walked into David's office on my first day at Sweet Darlings Inc.

Right now, the love of my life is lying on her stomach on our bed, writing snippets of code for a new feature she says is going to blow everyone's socks off. She transitioned to the app dev team after New Year's and does amazingly well there, as I knew she would. I adore the way her eyes sparkle when she talks about the new architecture (which I know nothing about, but who cares as long as she's happy) or the way she still flushes when I talk dirty to her. But most of all, I treasure her sweet, gentle heart—and the purity of a soul that keeps her humble and down to earth. Even after learning about her inheritance, she's the same lovable, vulnerable Jan I want to protect from the world.

"Your mom called earlier today," she says, still tapping away at her laptop.

"Did she?"

"Uh-huh. She said she's very sorry about being rude to me before, and that I should let you know she said so. You should call her. She sounded really unwell over the phone. Like she's been suffering from...uh...a severe case of constipation for the last few weeks."

I smirk. I told Mom in no uncertain terms that if she didn't apologize to Jan for the way she behaved, she could forget having me spend time with her. She probably didn't believe me—I've never held on to any anger with her for long. But my not going home for Thanksgiving and Christmas probably set her straight. (We spent the holidays with Jan's family, which was fun). I also didn't send her birthday flowers last week either. That most likely tipped the scale. One of the most aggressive lawyers I know, Mom hates to admit she did anything wrong. But she doesn't get to treat the love of my life badly and use the "Mom Card" to get away with it.

"You know what would be really cool?" Jan says, looking up from her laptop.

"What?"

"A trip to St. Cecilia. It's got the most gorgeous, romantic spot." She turns the screen, showing me an ad on Facebook. "Here."

I peer at it. It does look beautiful with pristine white beaches and emerald blue water. "I thought you were working," I tease, to hide my surprise since I was planning to take her there. Alexandra told me Jan has a valid passport, and I already got a week's vacation for both of us from Sweet Darlings Inc. for our Valentine's getaway, starting tomorrow. Sammi and Michelle already packed the things Jan's going to need at the resort since, as a guy, I know I'm going to forget something if I do it myself.

"Everyone needs to get away from time to time to recharge," Jan points out.

I grin. I forgot to mention another trait I adore about her—her newfound determination to value and treat herself better.

Unable to resist, I place the documents I've been reading on the bedside table and pull her toward me, palming her taut ass. "We can do that," I say. "We can do whatever you want."

"Really?" She gasps. Probably more from my fingers grazing over her braless nipple than my offer to do whatever she wants. Or maybe it's both. I really couldn't care less.

"Yes. Whatever, whenever." I pepper her neck with kisses, my dick swelling. I swear her scent is an aphrodisiac. If somebody could figure out a way to bottle it they'd make a fortune, easily outselling Viagra and Cialis combined.

Her gaze darkens, her breaths going shallow. "Then...shut up and kiss me."

"Your wish is my com—"

I spend the next…oh…at least a couple of hours engaged in the extraordinarily enjoyable act of pleasuring the most perfect woman in the world. Next time I'm inside her is going to be as her fiancé. I already bought a ring for the proposal in St. Cecilia. A yellow two-carat solitaire diamond on a platinum band. Its color reminds me of the sunflowers she loves so much, and I just knew it was the one when I saw it.

This man next door is going to be her man forever.

Thank you for reading *That Man Next Door*. I hope you liked it! The next book in Sweet Darlings Inc. is That Sexy Stranger, featuring Sammi! Join my mailing list at http://www.nadialee.net/newsletter to be notified when it's out!

The Billionaire's Forgotten Fiancée

The Billionaire's Forbidden Desire

The Billionaire's Holiday Bride

Seduced by the Billionaire

Taken by Her Unforgiving Billionaire Boss

Pursued by Her Billionaire Hook-Up

Pregnant with Her Billionaire Ex's Baby

Romanced by Her Illicit Millionaire Crush

Wanted by Her Scandalous Billionaire

Loving Her Best Friend's Billionaire Brother

ABOUT NADIA LEE

New York Times and *USA Today* bestselling author Nadia Lee writes sexy contemporary romance. Born with a love for excellent food, travel and adventure, she has lived in four different countries, kissed stingrays, been bitten by a shark, ridden an elephant and petted tigers.

Currently, she shares a condo overlooking a small river and sakura trees in Japan with her husband and son. When she's not writing, she can be found reading books by her favorite authors or planning another trip.

To learn more about Nadia and her projects, please visit http://www.nadialee.net. To receive updates about upcoming works from Nadia, please visit http://www.nadialee.net/newsletter to subscribe to her new release alert.

Stalk Me!

nadialee.net/newsletter
facebook.com/nadialeewrites